TRAGEDY
OF THE MOTH

SUZANNE MONDOUX

BALBOA.
PRESS
A DIVISION OF HAY HOUSE

Balboa Press books may be ordered through booksellers or by contacting:

Balboa Press
A Division of Hay House
1663 Liberty Drive
Bloomington, IN 47403
www.balboapress.com
1 (877) 407-4847

Print information available on the last page.

ISBN: 978-1-9822-2326-7 (sc)
ISBN: 978-1-9822-2327-4 (e)

Balboa Press rev. date: 03/05/2019

Contents

1

Elegant, desirably plump Felicity Moss sits on the edge of the tub, gazing at the razor in its charger. The early morning sun's rays shine through the window. Still in her evening gown, she reaches for the razor, looking into the mirror's reflection of the bedroom. She calls softly, "It's ready, my darling."

Alfred Manning stands in the bathroom entrance in an earnest manner. Standing He stands tall, shoulders back, fingers rubbing his chin. He turns to the window. Felicity removes the razor from the charger and hands it to him. He admires the way the light moves with her gown. She walks toward him and rubs the front and back of her hand on his unshaven cheeks. Still sleepy, he kisses her hand, takes the razor, and turns to face the mirror. She faces the mirror, too, raising her fingers to her face, gently following its shadows and lines.

"Time to return," she says sternly while glancing over at Alfred. She adds in a clean, clear tone, "Look at this, at us. These eyes."

Looking at the window, she hums a gentle tune. Alfred adjusts the razor for a close trim. Her face cream is next to him; he looks down at it and slides it to her.

"Thank you, my darling," she says briskly. "Don't forget to put the razor back in the charger when you're done."

Placing the razor against his cheek, he watches her wash her face, admiring each movement of the cloth against her perfectly smooth, firm, olive skin.

"When are we going on that trip?" she asks in her clean, clear timbre. "Will you come if we travel to the mountains?"

Brushing her short, black hair, and with giving a delightful laugh, she walks into the bedroom. Posturing along the edge of the bed, she continues brushing her hair. Alfred follows, sits next to her, and continues to shave.

"Tell me, my darling: how long will Samuel stay in the beach house?"

He turns off the razor, takes the brush from her, and continues brushing her hair.

"I'm not certain." He holds her hand and puts it against his cheek for her inspection. "How was he with you?" he asks in a begrudging tone.

"Samuel was a gentleman, my darling. We danced all night only because you were engaged elsewhere. Besides, I believe he loves another."

Curious, Alfred leans back onto the bed. "Oh? What makes you say that?" Felicity leans into Alfred with a loving embrace.

"Woman's intuition, my love. It's just the way he was. I can't quite put my finger on it. When I asked him about the ladies in his life, he just shrugged his shoulders. He said he's taking a sabbatical from dating. Are you aware that Samuel hasn't been on a date since you introduced me to him? Remember, it was the weekend that Rose was with us at the beach house. She came to see how I was doing before she left for Africa. It was Christmas 2007. She and Luc were very close. It was the second anniversary of his—"

He kisses her with a full embrace. "Next time, it's just you and I who'll go dancing." Alfred gets up from the bed to get his jacket. Reaching into its pocket, he pulls out a photo. "What a sight!" he scoffs. "This lunatic with his arm around my shoulder, pretending to be my best friend. Can you believe it? Rose is back in Africa, isn't she? Why didn't Samuel go with her? He only went that one time. He hasn't been back since."

"He *is* your best friend," says Felicity as she takes the photo for a closer look.

"The last time Samuel and I spent this much time together was in boarding school in England. I was fifteen when my parents told me we had to move to Canada." Alfred walks to the open window and looks out. "The sea is calm today. Let's go sailing."

"He danced with me all night. He has an opinionated yet seductive stare. Does he know?"

"Felicity, you are the female version of the character in Camus's *The Stranger*—you are Meursault in many ways. Your choice made you appear indifferent to humankind, a soulless mother incapable of mourning the death of her child, who died at her hands. You had a choice to make, and you chose love and your compassion for life to save Luc. You did what he desired. Assisted suicide was his choice. Your choice will not be revered but shunned by those who feel and believe that they must live in judgment of others. You unwillingly live your life as you see it must be, not by those who tell you how it should be. Remorse is not an emotion you accept, and for this you will always, as Meursault did, await your death while others try to direct you to repent and atone with God. It is their ignorance, my love, that blinds them from seeing that you never turned away from God but toward him, which is what gave you the strength and courage to give your son his final wish."

She remembers finding Luc on the floor, covered with vomit and shit, begging her to kill him. His bed was soaked with blood-red piss. She recalls how she felt, her will to keep him alive broken. How she drew him a bath, and he screamed for her to kill him. How she remained silent as she removed his clothing. Dragging him to the bathroom and lifting his heavy body into the tub, strapping him in so he didn't sink into the now-soiled water and drown.

A confused Luc, hoping she would let him drown, screamed with frustration. "I fucking hate you! Why are you doing this to me? Fucking kill me!"

Felicity, in her silence, walked back into the room to clean the bed. Her head back, she took long inhales, holding her breath to avoid the stench that burned her nostrils. Back in the bathroom, she lifted Luc out of the tub and onto a towel on the floor. Luc was filled with hate toward his mother for not letting him drown. She dried him as he continued crying for her to help him.

"Mommy, why?"

Her eighteen-year-old son wept like a child. She dragged him to his room, still on the towel, and lifted him onto the clean bed.

"I'll be right back, Luc."

She left the room. A few minutes later, she returned with a bottle of medication in one hand and a letter in the other. Luc stopped crying and went silent. The letter, written by Luc with the assistance of his lawyer, stated that he had requested assisted suicide to end his life because of the pain and suffering he had endured for the past two years due to kidney cancer that had spread to his bones. Felicity placed the pills and the letter on the night table next to the bed. She sat next to Luc. She opened the bottle, poured the pills into a glass, crushed them, and added juice to take away the bitter taste.

"Thank you, Mother!"

She placed the glass to his mouth. Luc drank with relief.

"I think you left some of your sailing clothes here last time," Alfred says, his gaze still on the sea.

Felicity is jolted back to the present.

"My shoes," she responds as she looks down at her bare feet, her toenails painted light pink. "I took them off because they got wet when I got off the boat, when we docked on the island last time. Did I bring them back to your place, or did I forget them on the beach? I don't remember wearing them when we got back on the boat."

"I carried them back for you. You were a bit drunk, so you don't remember. I left them on the porch next to the Adirondack chair you built for me."

Alfred turns to Felicity with a smile on his face, as though remembering that wonderful day on the island.

"That lunatic Samuel, my love—I wouldn't worry about him. He says that all women—especially beautiful ones like you—are, from what he has learned from Scandinavian folklore, huldras. The huldra is a seductive forest creature whose name derives from a root meaning 'secret.' The huldra is believed to have the mystical power of luring men into the forest to have sexual intercourse with her. These men would be rewarded if they satisfied her or killed if they did not. Or, in some cases, the huldra forced the man to marry her."

Alfred raises his hand to his head, stroking his dark, full hair away from his forehead. His reflection in the full-length mirror mounted on the wall across the room reveals the shape of time. His midforties have presented a new challenge. Extra time at the gym and jogs on the beach to melt away those hard-to-burn fat cells around his midsection were now necessary to maintain the once-effortless sculpted body of his youth.

"As I said," he goes on, "Samuel is a weird chap. He acts as though he is your conscience. He holds himself at an extraordinary high status in his mind. I think he suffers from delusions of grandeur, despite the fact that he's extremely wealthy. He comes from old money, is extremely brilliant, and holds two PhDs—one in philosophy, the other in theology. He's fit and good-looking. Women love him, and so do men. But as I said, he's a lunatic! He's never made a donation in his life and never lends money to anyone. He also doesn't gamble and never takes any financial risks. But he somehow, after his parents died, multiplied the family wealth more than his father ever could have done when he was alive. I don't know how he did it. Every cent is honest money. Pays his taxes and never cheats the government or anyone. He doesn't even look for tax breaks." Alfred takes Felicity into his arms and dances around the room with her. "Let's go sailing. We can pick up what we need in town and have lunch on the boat. The *Magdalene* can stretch her legs. We'll take her out of the channel."

Felicity, released from Alfred's hold, continues to glide from the momentum of the spin until she reaches the closet door.

"You know him well," she says. "Samuel misses you. I could see it in his face. You are all he has."

Opening the closet door, she looks up toward the top shelf for a day bag to pack towels and swimsuits in. She removes her evening gown by letting it slide down along her body to the floor.

The sunlight reveals her exquisite, full figure as a shadow gliding as though projected from behind the closet wall.

"I'll bring our wool jumpers in case we decide to stay out longer. We can watch the sunset from the Henderson family's seafood restaurant. Let's avoid the club for a while."

As she reaches up for the jumpers, a shadow from behind encapsulates her body with an amatory glow. Alfred carries Felicity to their bed. As the sun continues to rise, casting a stream of shadows across the room, Alfred and Felicity rediscover each other.

"Well done, Mr. Manning. The huldra is quite satisfied. You've outdone yourself once again. I don't think I shall kill you today." Felicity moves gently from Alfred's embrace, motioning him to roll onto his back.

"I am pleased to have satisfied the huldra. I am at your service." Alfred laughs as he asks, "What do you have against the club?"

Felicity, straddling him, lets the breeze from the open windows cool her body. Looking down at him, breathless, she coos, "Do you remember when I first met you on the beach? I was walking in the waves as they came up. The trial had just ended. It was on the one-year anniversary of Luc's death."

Not remembering the details, Alfred gives her a forgetful look, shrugging his shoulders with eyebrows closing in on each other, and says, "I don't remember meeting you on the beach."

"You were on your balcony, fixing your chair, and saw me walking. I was technically within your property line. You called out to me and walked over to me. You asked why I had not taken off my shoes to walk in the water. You then said I looked familiar but you couldn't think of where we may have met. You invited me for a drink. You closed up the house, and we drove to the club. Before going in, you gave me the grand tour and introduced me to the *Magdalene*. You invited me to go sailing that afternoon because you had just done some maintenance work on her and wanted to take her out to see how she was doing. But we never did go out that afternoon because…" Felicity's words trail off as Alfred brings her close to him, caressing her with his most endearing tone.

"Never mind them," he says.

"Those people recognized me immediately, but you had no idea who I was—not immediately, anyway. When we sat at the bar to order drinks, one of the club members—can't remember his name—asked you who I was. You said you had found me wandering on the beach without knowing if I was coming or going. He returned to his companion, and then they both turned and stared at me. Later, when you went off to the men's room, that man followed you. When you came out, I knew he had reminded you of where you thought you recognized my face from. It didn't take him long to spread the word in the club, and before you knew it, everyone was staring. A year prior, I had been on trial for the murder of my son, which was broadcast on every news channel across the world. I was inundated by a world of judgment."

Alfred gets up, taking Felicity with him, and walks to the balcony doors. Swinging them open, he walks her out onto the balcony overlooking the sea. Her cheeks are flushed, and she can smell the salt air.

Alfred embraces Felicity and says, "They see your choice as an offense. That just may be their offense. We cannot avoid the club or places associated with our painful memories. Death has its place. It was served to you on a platter."

> Love is a strange and wonderful thing.
> Love dances with our hearts,
> Plays with our fears,
> Adds color to our world.
> It shares our sorrows and joys,
> Blinds us with wonder,
> Allows us to grow.
> It's a challenge of faith,
> A journey of hope, and is
> Often-uncharted waters.
> What a ride!

"Luc gave you the ride of your life," Alfred says. "There's more to come. Let's get dressed."

Felicity stares off into space. Luc had been playing on the beach, laughing, when suddenly he was thrown from one wave to another, all the while hanging on to his shorts for dear life. It was the first time he had forgotten to bring his bucket and shovel; sand castles were a thing of the past. Impressing the girls while trying not to drown or die from embarrassment had become the challenge.

In her one-piece swimsuit with a tiny skirt elegantly adapted to her body, Felicity watched from her Adirondack chair. Her large yellow sun hat, the brim greater than the width of her shoulders, concealed the lowering of her book at every line so as not to lose sight of Luc. Suddenly, at a distance, she could see a large wave forming and traveling at a speed faster than he could swim. She sat up in her chair, dropping the book in the sand, and then got up, shouting out to him to swim as fast as he could. The wave picked up speed, volume, and height with such intensity, eating everything in its path. Luc was gone.

"No!" Felicity white-knuckles the balcony railing.

"What do you mean, no?" Alfred calls out from inside. "Does my huldra wish to go sailing unclothed?"

The ocean's glitter redirects her focus. Releasing the railing, her attention is drawn to the sounds of the seals sunning themselves on the large rock at the foot of the cove.

"Can you get me my long-sleeved blue shirt with white-trimmed collar and blue pants?" she says. "They're hanging on the far left, next to your work shirts."

The early autumn sun is rising over the mountains, and the air carries a light breeze, leaving Felicity with a gentle shiver of tiny goose bumps on her olive skin. The blissful sea maneuvers the composition of the waves, executing a flawless waltz. Felicity takes the knitted, umber-colored blanket hanging over the chair next to her and wraps it over her shoulders. A chill of frost felt, she looks down at her feet.

"I mustn't forget my boat shoes," she says quietly to herself.

"Felicity, your clothes are on the bed. Get dressed, my love. Let's make the most of the day." Alfred's plea, filled with excitement for the day ahead out at sea, is muffled by an electric toothbrush head's rapid oscillation against his teeth, followed by gurgling and spitting sounds. "Your shoes, my love. Don't forget your shoes outside, by the chair." Alfred walks out of the bathroom, drying his face with a towel.

Felicity, wrapped in the blanket, which hangs down past her feet, gives the illusion that she is gliding into the room. Shivering, she turns to close the doors, looking out onto where she has left her memory of the sea.

"Honey, here's your clothes. I love these colors on you." Alfred takes the clothes he laid on the bed and hands them to her. "Swap?"

Felicity, with a winglike motion, removes the blanket from her body.

"Thank you," she says with love in her eyes as she takes the clothes he holds against his body, which is naked except for the towel thrown over his shoulder. "It will only take me a minute to get ready. Don't forget to get the jumpers from the closet, Alfred. They fell on the floor."

"Our sunglasses and gloves and everything else we need are already on the boat," he says. "Out of the sea will rise Behemoth and Leviathan, and sail 'round the high-pooped galleys…"

Amused by his playful accent, she responds, "I'm ready, Oscar Wilde. We can go."

Alfred scoops up the cardigans from the closet floor and with a skip and a hop, leaps to the bedroom doors and opens them with enthusiasm.

"Good morning!" calls out Samuel. "It's about time you two got up."

The fervor in Alfred's step vanishes as quickly as the light is blown from a candle. "Samuel, what the hell are you doing here?" Alfred looks back at Felicity with his arms thrown in the air in disbelief. She takes the jumpers from him and throws them on the bed.

"Did you forget I was here?" Samuel is stretched out on the sofa with a cup of coffee, reading the paper. He sits up and, in a confident but challenging voice, baits Alfred. "And good morning to you, too!" Seeing Felicity, he softens and says, "Good morning, my lovely Felicity. How are you today? Lovely morning, don't you think?"

"What the fuck, Samuel?" Alfred walks sternly toward the sofa. "You were supposed to be gone before we got up. I know you have an office, and I think you can afford a place of your own."

"Yeah, but I like it here. Why would I want to stay anywhere else? This is the best beach house on the coast. While we're all here, let me make you breakfast." Eager to please, he gets up off the couch to greet them both with kisses. "Would you like to start with a lovely home-brewed cup of coffee?"

Alfred places his hands on his hips in an attempt to assert his authority in his own house. "For fuck's sake, Samuel, put on some clothes!"

Samuel wraps the *Daily Journal* around himself to lessen the offense.

"My God!" Alfred fumes. "I can't believe this!" He takes Felicity by the hand and walks toward the front door. "Samuel, we have plans today. Felicity and I are going sailing all day and then out for dinner. We won't be back until later tonight."

Felicity walks back to the bedroom to get the jumpers. "What did you have in mind for breakfast?" she asks Samuel. "Honey, we do need to eat something before we go."

"Now, that's better. A little bit of gratitude. Hostility only equals stress, Alfred." Samuel throws the paper on the sofa. "I'll be right back. Don't go anywhere. Breakfast will be ready in no time."

Alfred's frustration is even further compounded by a knock at the door.

"Now, who could that be at this time of the morning?" Alfred's compass is set, and he senses it will no doubt be readjusted, and it will be a futile attempt to try to keep his plans on course. He can only hope that the remains of the day allow him to chart a course on the *Magdalene*.

"Good morning, Mr. Manning," a voice calls from behind the door. "It's Mrs. Hitchcock from the bakery. I have your order."

"Hitchcock? What order?" Alfred, not moving, resigns himself to the day ahead of him.

"Honey, let her in." Felicity points a finger at the door.

He opens it as instructed. There stands a woman with bluish-gray hair tied back in a bun. A wrinkled face maps her journey from here to there. Her body curves from east to west. And held in her dried, knobby-knuckled hands is a white bag, with the inscription "Hitchcock Buns," releasing an aroma of freshly made baked goods.

"Good morning, Mr. Manning. Lovely to see you again." She smiles and quickly explains her presence. "I got a call this morning. He said his name was Samuel. He said he's a friend of yours and was staying at the beach house. He said it would be nice to have fresh bread and pastries this morning and asked if I wouldn't mind making a delivery."

"Thank you, Mrs. Hitchcock, that's very kind of you to go out of your way," Alfred says. "I hope it wasn't too much trouble."

"Not at all, Mr. Manning," she exclaims, redirecting her gaze at the man walking toward her. "Good morning. How are you today?"

"I'm just wonderful! You must be Mrs. Hitchcock. You look lovely this morning. Allow me to introduce myself. I'm Samuel," he says, putting out his hand.

"Ah, thank you, Mr. Samuel. Here's the order you placed. Would you like me to cut the bread and put the pastries on a dish for you?"

"That would be lovely—"

"No! Mrs. Hitchcock, please," Alfred pleads. "Do not bother yourself." He frowns at Samuel.

"Please, Mrs. Hitchcock, allow me." Felicity gracefully leaps toward her and takes the bakery bag from her.

"Allow me to introduce Felicity Moss, Mrs. Hitchcock," says Alfred.

"Yes, Samuel mentioned you had a friend with you. It's lovely to make your acquaintance, Mrs. Moss."

Alfred cringes at the thought of Samuel keeping Mrs. Hitchcock interested with tales of this and that surrounding his personal life.

"Please, call me Felicity, Mrs. Hitchcock. It's lovely to make your acquaintance as well."

"Would you like a cup of coffee, Mrs. Hitchcock?" offers Samuel as he gestures toward the kitchen table. "Please, take a seat."

"Oh please, if it's no bother."

Samuel takes her by the hand and directs her to a chair. "Please, sit here, Mrs. Hitchcock." He pulls out the chair and tucks her back in at the table.

"Milk? Sugar?" he asks.

"Milk, please."

"May I offer you one of these great pastries, Mrs. Hitchcock? The baker comes highly recommended," he says with a wink. Samuel takes the bag from Felicity. He gestures with his hand to both her and Alfred. "Please, have a seat while I get the coffee ready."

Alfred reluctantly takes a seat while Felicity goes to help Samuel.

"Samuel, have a seat," Felicity implores as she takes the bag from him. She gently grabs him by the shoulders and turns him around toward the table.

"Lovely. I'll sit next to Mrs. Hitchcock," says Samuel.

Alfred, restless in his chair, keeps looking outside and realizes that Mrs. Hitchcock's car isn't there.

"How did you get here, Mrs. Hitchcock?" Leaning back in his chair, he points toward the driveway.

"I walked, Mr. Manning. It's a lovely morning."

"You walked all the way from the bakery? That's more than two miles. Felicity and I will drive you back to the bakery. We're going into town and can drop you on the way."

"That would be lovely, Mr. Manning. Thank you."

Felicity returns to the table with a tray of baked goods, cut bread, butter, and jams.

"Honey, can you get the coffee cups and coffee, please?" she asks Alfred.

He gets up from the table and returns with cups and coffee. As he is about to set them down, Samuel leans forward, with elbows on the table, getting in Alfred's way, and directs his attention to Mrs. Hitchcock.

"Tell me, are you related to Alfred Hitchcock?"

Alfred just about dropped everything on the floor and nudged Samuel for both getting in his way and asking a personal question of Mrs. Hitchcock.

"No, I'm not related to Alfred Hitchcock," she replies. "Hitchcock was my husband's name. He died in the war. I left England shortly after to come live with my sister. I needed help with my children. It was difficult for women to find work when the men returned home after the war ended. My sister had settled on the West Coast with her husband. He was a schoolteacher. Back then, this part of the coast was very remote and isolated from other cities and communities. It was difficult to get teachers out here. He had a friend who had come to Canada a few years prior as a teacher as well but worked in Montreal. He wrote him and mentioned in his letter that teachers were needed on the West Coast, north of Tofino. A few months later, my sister and her husband arrived. They lived for forty years in the house around the bend, just past the big rock."

"Yes, that's a lovely old, big house," says Samuel. "Are they still there?"

"No. George died five years ago and Martha eight years ago." Mrs. Hitchcock sips her coffee after she finishes her sentence.

"I'm sorry, Mrs. Hitchcock." Samuel offers her a pastry.

"Thank you." She accepts it, grateful for the attention.

Samuel, still inquisitive, continues with his interrogation. "Was your husband related to Alfred Hitchcock, then?"

"No, afraid not."

"How many children did you have when you came to Tofino, Mrs. Hitchcock?"

Alfred addresses Samuel with his eyes, giving him a stern look. "Let's not tire Mrs. Hitchcock with all these questions after she just walked more than two miles to bring us these lovely pastries. Let her enjoy her coffee and eat in peace. I'm sure you must be tired, Mrs. Hitchcock."

She finishes chewing and sips her coffee. "Thank you, Mr. Manning."

"Please, Mrs. Hitchcock, call me Alfred."

Felicity raises the coffeepot, ready to pour. "Would you like more, Mrs. Hitchcock?"

"Yes, please. Thank you, Mrs. Moss."

"Call me Felicity."

"You have a lovely home, Mr. Manning. Alfred," Mrs. Hitchcock corrects herself as she looks around the room.

"Thank you," he replies. "It took some time to build because of the details, but it was worth the wait. It was important to have the house blend with the natural environment as much as possible and for it to be welcoming. I also didn't want a mansion, despite the large property. I wanted comfortable yet spacious and ended up with what you see today."

"You did a wonderful job, Alfred. I think—"

Samuel cuts Mrs. Hitchcock off, leaning toward her. "Would you like a tour? It has a lovely view of the cove from the bedrooms and, on the other side, the sea as far as the eye can see."

"I can see you, Samuel, and that's as far as that." Mrs. Hitchcock points at her glasses, resting on the tip of her nose.

"Great. Let's go for a tour. I'll bring the binoculars."

Alfred, now completely resigned to the fact that he's not going anywhere anytime soon, still reminds Felicity about her footwear.

"Don't forget your shoes before we go. Let's accompany Mrs. Hitchcock on her tour."

Samuel helps Mrs. Hitchcock out of her chair, presents his arm like the gentlemen he is, and directs her to the back of the house. "Let's go see the cove. You can see the seals on the rocks."

Everyone makes his way to the U-shaped beach that wraps around the property. A deep, massive forest covers the remaining part.

Samuel is still intrigued by finding out how this sweet little old lady could be related to Alfred Hitchcock. Unable to help himself, he continues the probing questions. "Mrs. Hitchcock…"

As perceptive as he is about Samuel, Alfred sees that he is about to launch into a fit of questions and decides to intervene. "Mrs. Hitchcock, please let me know when you are ready to return to the bakery. I don't want to take any more of your time."

"Thank you, Alfred. I am feeling tired." Before making a move, she turns to address Felicity. "Mrs. Moss, tell me, have we met before? You look terribly familiar. Have you been in my bakery?"

The sea pounding against the shore is amplified in the sudden silence. Felicity regains herself when Alfred puts his arm around her, and she cautiously responds, "No, I don't think I've been in your bakery, Mrs. Hitchcock. I don't think we've met before."

"I'm sure I've seen your face somewhere," she insists.

"I must just have one of those familiar faces. I look like many people."

Mrs. Hitchcock raises her hand, tapping her finger to her head. With a sudden realization, she excitedly responds, "I know where I've seen your face."

Everyone freezes with anticipation. A knot forms in Felicity's stomach. She likes Mrs. Hitchcock and doesn't want to think that this lovely old lady could be part of the jury that would sooner sentence her to death by hanging or throw her into the sea with hands bound and rocks tied to her feet than give her a fair trial.

"I saw you at my sister's house," Mrs. Hitchcock says.

Everyone stood there, looking confused.

"I'm sorry, Mrs. Hitchcock," says Felicity. "I don't think I've ever met your sister either."

"Yes. You are in her photo album," Mrs. Hitchcock insists.

"How do you mean?"

"You're that actress. My sister was your photographer."

"Are you saying that Martha Wilson is your sister?" Felicity, verging on hysterical laughter as the knot in her stomach releases, quickly regains her composure.

"Yes, that's her. A few years after George began working, Martha decided to take up a hobby she had put aside while looking after her two children. While they were at school all day, she started taking photos of people in the community and at the school. She was then asked to take photos at weddings, parties, and—well, what can I say? The rest is history."

To bring Alfred up to speed, Felicity explains the connection. "Alfred, Martha was known as the top photographer in North America. She definitely was the best. She mentioned that she had a place on the coast, but I didn't know any more than that. She was a very private person. Her work was her work, but her homelife was her own."

"Yes, that was Martha," agreed Mrs. Hitchcock.

"Well, now that we have all that cleared up, let's continue our tour." Samuel offers her his arm once again.

"Thank you, Samuel, but I think it's time I return to my bakery. The staff is going to wonder where I am."

As slow and graceful as a drifting feather, Mrs. Hitchcock turns from the sea and begins heading for the front of the house, thinking to herself that Felicity is as beautiful in person as she is in the photographs taken by Martha.

Felicity gently places her arm around Mrs. Hitchcock. "I'll drive you."

"But we didn't get a chance to look at the seals sitting on one of the Eustand horses," cries Samuel as he points the other way.

"What do you mean, sitting on one of the Eustand horses?" Alfred says, clearly annoyed.

"Have you not heard of the legendary horse of Eustand?" goads Samuel, rolling his eyes.

Alfred, quickly losing patience, directs Mrs. Hitchcock toward his car. Samuel ignores Alfred's gesture to shut up and walks toward the sea, pointing at an island far in the distance.

"Look, over there!" His arm is stretched straight as an arrow, with his finger pointing as though he's able to reach out and touch the island. "Since you are not familiar with the local legend, Alfred, I will have to educate you. Eustand was a monk who lived on the island—that one out there. He was alone except for ten wild horses that resided on the island with him. These horses were not like all the other horses. Their colors and their names were different. These horses were the colors of the rainbow, and each was named after one of the Ten Commandments. Life on the island was peaceful. Everything, every thought, was in harmony with nature and each other. One day, the sea turned gray; the dark sky and the sea were one. The wind ferociously tossed towers of waves onto the island. Eustand and the horses believed God had released his vengeance on them for their sin. But what sin? None of them knew that a sin had been committed. They spent the night huddled together in a cave. Thunder rattled the island. The ferocity of each lightning strike illuminated the entire island. All they could do was to wait out the storm until morning."

"Samuel, we don't have time for this," shouted Alfred. "I plan on going sailing today, and I don't want to miss it. Mrs. Hitchcock needs to get home. She's already been put out enough. My apologies, Mrs. Hitchcock. Let me help you into the car."

Not fazed in the least, Samuel shrugs his shoulders and heads for the car.

"I'm curious, Samuel," says Mrs. Hitchcock. "What was the sin, and which of the ten horses turned to stone?"

"Thou shalt not kill, Mrs. Hitchcock."

The slamming of the car door echoes throughout the forest. Alfred walks toward Samuel, who quickly shuffles away from the fury before him. Suddenly, the scream of a coast guard siren snaps Alfred out of his murderous rage. They turn to see the boat racing up the coastline, the siren announcing that there is a man overboard. Just up around the bend, there's a 200-meter cliff waiting for its next victim. In spite of the danger and the inevitable disastrous outcome, the vast splendor of Devil's Chin's panoramic view lures its prey along the precipice, tempting the person to take that one last step to see what's there, just out of reach.

Alfred runs to where his binoculars are hanging on the back porch. He leaps, unhooks them in one sweep, and races off to the edge of the shore. Samuel is in tow, leaving Mrs. Hitchcock and Felicity sitting in the car.

"It looks like it's just us girls, Mrs. Hitchcock," Felicity quips as she gets out of the backseat and into the driver's seat.

"I hope no one is hurt," says Mrs. Hitchcock as she looks in the direction of the sirens.

"I'm sure no one is," Felicity says, trying to assuage Mrs. Hitchcock's concern.

2

"Justin, what went through your mind when you raised the sword?" Felicity asks her acting student.

"I wanted to kill him," replies Justin.

"What did you feel?"

"Anger. Hurt. I'm not sure, Mrs. Moss."

"Why?"

Justin stands silent on stage, pondering who Edward, his character, really is. He read the script over and over and over again before coming to class. He doesn't want to disappoint Felicity. She had taken a few years off work to create a small theater school a few miles up the coast. For the past two years in a row, she's had the same eleven committed students.

"What does Edward want?" Felicity, holding the script, turns back the pages.

Justin stares down at his sixteenth-century boots, twirling the tip of his sword on the ground. Confused, he looks up at Felicity. "Forgiveness?" Then, more confidently, "He wants forgiveness."

"That's right," says Felicity as she sits back in her chair. Pointing at the sword, she continues her direction. "Do it again, from there."

Edward is at the mercy of his opponent. The sword swings of its own will, diving into the stage floor.

"Justin," Felicity calls out.

Justin falls to his knees, exhausted.

"What did that feel like?" asks Felicity.

"Like Edward. I think I know who he is now." He walks to the edge of the stage. He sits, legs dangling, with the sword on his lap.

"I want you to prepare the same scene again for next week. But we're also going to add the next two scenes. Edward will be faced with a choice. Good work!" Redirecting her focus to another student, Felicity continues, "Sabrina, you're up next." She leans forward to take the next script from her bag. She turns the pages for a minute while Sabrina waits onstage.

"I see you finished writing your play," says Felicity as she looks up at Sabrina.

"It's still a draft, Mrs. Moss. I wanted to see what it would be like—"

"Great uniform. Where did you get it?" interrupts Felicity.

"It belonged to my grandmother. She was a nurse in World War Two."

"What will you read for us today?"

"A monologue." She beams. "Well, it's not really a monologue. It's a letter written by one of the soldiers my grandmother…He died. In this letter was a poem: 'Remembering the Soldiers.'"

"Whenever you're ready," Felicity says.

> Let me tell you the story of a soldier who lay facedown in a trench. Covered in mud, cold and stiff, his corpse emitted a scent carried with each breeze. A large bullet hole parted his back, drenched in mud, staining his skin rusty red. Cradled next to him was his comrade, with tears rolling down his cheeks.
>
> Frozen with fear, afraid to die, he stayed hidden until sunrise.
>
> The morning mist dropped crystals on each blade of grass. The cool air woke him, reminding him where he was. He slowly rose to take a peek at the war and saw a ship docked at sea. Not remembering the sea was so

close, he crawled out from the trench, toward the ship, to climb aboard.

He met the captain and asked, "What is our destination?"

The captain replied, "Heaven, of course."

Facedown, dead, and cold, comfort to another soul.

Loud and clear, death is here, returning some to their homes.

Memories following the lost souls; suicide cut out their hope.

Dedicated to all the soldiers who did not return and to those who could not stay.

The room remains silent as Sabrina recites the last words ever written by a soldier, a boy of eighteen years.

"Well done, Sabrina," says Felicity as she straightens herself in her chair. "Next week I want you to take this script instead. Then we'll go back to yours."

The mood needs to be lightened with a bit of comic relief, and Felicity knows just who to call up next.

"Arnold, you're up. What do you have for us today?" She waits in anticipation.

"*The Man in the Hamper*, Mrs. Moss," he replies with a straight face.

"Sounds interesting. Whenever you're ready." She motions with a wave of her hand.

Arnold dances around the stage, and everyone laughs out loud, bent over, stomachs cramped. At the end of the scene, Arnold receives a standing ovation. Quite pleased with himself, he takes a long, stretched bow, ending with a curtsy as the final touch.

As he looks up, he sees the clock in the corner of the room and shouts, "I gotta run. Kayak lessons begin in fifteen minutes." He jumps off the stage, grabs his bag, and waves his long arms at his classmates. Realizing that they all take kayaking lessons together, they follow Arnold and run out—all except for Sabrina.

"Sabrina, it's a lovely day. Why are you not going with the rest of them?" Felicity walks up on the stage to rearrange the props.

"My play, Mrs. Moss. I would like to discuss my play."

"What exactly would you like to discuss?"

"God," Sabrina says sincerely.

"What about God?"

"That's it, Mrs. Moss. What about God?" Sabrina sits in a chair, placing her bag next to it.

Felicity, still onstage, continues to question her. "Tell me what you understand of God, Sabrina."

"I must be good, or else God will punish me," Sabrina says.

"What else?" Felicity probes.

"Every time I do something good, I get a rose waiting for me in heaven."

"Then you should have a beautiful rose garden by now, Sabrina." Felicity sits on the stage steps.

"Well, that's just it. I'm not sure. I mean, I don't understand what good I'm supposed to do or when I've done something bad. I mean, of course I know when I've done something I'm not supposed to, like telling a lie, cursing—you know, the basics. But I remember when I was smaller, our school would take us to church for confession. I couldn't think of anything I had to confess, so I lied."

"What do you mean, Sabrina?"

"I mean that because I couldn't think of any sin I had committed since my last confession, which was about a week, I would make things up. I would lie to the priest just so he would see I was a good girl by confessing my sins. I was making up sins. How screwed up is that? So I doubt I was getting a rose for that bit."

"Probably not, but do you really think God's definition of sin is the same as what we have come to believe it is?"

Not sure what to think of that question, Sabrina, wiggling in her chair, asks, "What do you mean?"

"What you know about God now—is it the same you knew of God then?"

Sabrina still looks confused. Felicity continues, "Let me ask you this instead. Soon you'll be starting college, to study archaeology. This has been your passion since you were a little girl, and you've read just about every archaeology book to prepare yourself. At school you ask questions about this and that. When did you realize, starting from when you were just a wee little girl and through the passing years, that your Catholic teachings clashed with the scientific findings of which you were told? How did you feel when you realized that, yes, Jesus may have been married and had children? Let alone that he was married to Mary Magdalene, and so on. Also what if Jesus asked Judah to betray him? Maybe Jesus may have had his own motives for how he wanted the events of that night to play out. Maybe getting himself crucified was part of his plan, and the only way to do so was to have Judah do what he asked."

"It was only a couple years ago that I realized I did not believe what I was taught," confesses Sabrina. "In a moment, I knew all that was shit. And what's strange about it was that God spoke to me. One night, while in bed, I decided to pray. I realized I had not said a prayer in a very long time. I wanted God to help me with my play—yes, this one, the one I've been working on for two years now. And it was in that moment that it all became clear to me. I love God. My relationship with him or her or whatever—we'll say 'him' for the sake of argument—is very personal, and I don't want anyone butting in, if you know what I mean."

"Yes, I do." Felicity takes Sabrina's play from her bag. "Now, this work, Sabrina, is wonderful. The one recommendation I can offer is that you rewrite the entire play and remember who you are. Write about the woman you thought you knew and transform her into the woman she really is."

Felicity feels a vibration next to her feet. She looks down at her bag, and her phone shimmies under the fabric.

"It's a lovely day, Sabrina. Go kayaking with the rest of them. Enjoy the day." Felicity fumbles for her phone and waves Sabrina off.

She looks down at the name on the caller ID: Jack Saunders, her manager. She sits in her chair, pondering whether she wants to answer or not. She has not seen or spoken with Jack since the media got hold of her story, and she told Jack she was taking time away from the big screen.

A memory flashes in her mind. Sitting behind his desk, smoking a cigar, Jack stared at her for what felt like hours before he spoke. He scratched his ginger-haired head, reflecting the light from the window behind him.

"Tell me, young lady, how is it that we don't know about you?"

Felicity shyly smiled at him. He put out his cigar in a large glass ashtray placed within perfect reach.

"My apologies. It's rude of me to be puffing away in here when we have such a young, healthy person in the office." He played around with his scruffy beard. "Felicity, you and I are going to work together for a very long time, and to celebrate, here's the manuscript I want you to study. Audition's tomorrow morning at nine." Writing on the cover, he added, "This is the address. Don't be late. I'll be there as well."

Felicity stared at the portrait of Oscar Wilde hanging on the far left wall. Jack followed her gaze.

"No, I didn't know him personally." He smiled at her. She giggled and took the manuscript with the audition address from his desk.

"Thank you, Mr. Saunders. I'll see you tomorrow."

"It's Jack."

The buzzing phone brings her back to the present. She presses the green Answer button.

"Well, it's about time you answered your phone. Where the fuck are you?"

"Good to hear your voice as well, Jack," Felicity says with a laugh.

"Honey, it's been a while, and I have a project for you that I don't want you to miss out on. How are you? We all miss you. I hear you opened up an acting school. We don't want to lose you to those kids I've been hearing about. We haven't talked since…"

"You should come over and meet some of them. It would be your opportunity to impress and torment a new generation of young actors."

"Honey, I'm always up for that, but I'm too busy. I e-mailed you the manuscript; it's a doozy! Promise me you'll read it tonight and call me back tomorrow."

"What's it about?" asks Felicity in a suspicious tone.

"Come on, don't be like that." He blows out a puff of smoke.

"Can you give me an idea?" Felicity hears her students messing around in the kayaks and the bursts of laughter when one of them calls out that Arnold has capsized again. "You still smoke those cigars, Jack? They will be the death of you. I'm surprised you're not already pushing tulips."

"Funny you should mention tulips. Read the manuscript and call me tomorrow. I have to run. Kiss, kiss, Felicity."

She looks down at the phone, the call ended. She can still hear her students laughing. Arnold has not drowned yet; cheers ring out for his clumsy recovery.

❖ ❖ ❖

Toes on the limits of the precipice, her mind wanders. She looks down at the trees protruding as though in suspension, fighting gravity. Could one be in suspension, denying gravity its chance to motion toward the ground, crushing the body? Contemplating other options, the arid soil carried by the breeze grimly massages her body while the wind's voice fills her ears; the only choice is to jump. Nothing can keep her from staying. She listens closely to the sound of the grit at her feet. Tiny sand particles scratch her cheeks when she turns her head to look around, searching for a way out, but the air is smooth when she looks directly down to where she will land if she lets herself fall over.

It is early morning, and the sun is beginning to rise. She feels at ease. She wants to spread her wings and fly like a bird. She knows her landing will not be as elegant. The thought causes her to hesitate. She cannot help but think how her choice will tarnish the pristine wilderness below. What kind of mess will she leave? The outcome will be a splattered body at the base of this majestic cliff—not the legacy she wants to leave behind for her children, for nature. But she still wants to jump. There is nothing else to do. She has reviewed all other options. There is only one other that seems hopeful, but in the end, after a second look, she knows the option to jump is the best one.

This is how Felicity remembers the story ending, yet she's unsure how it began. She can remember only bits and pieces of it. When she tells this story, she wonders what would happen if she remembered it all. How different things would be if she actually remembered the beginning. Would knowing change the ending? She's skeptical of it all. It's as if time did not pass. What kind of quantum leap had she just made? The quantum aspect of her life is the eeriest part of her entire existence. How many quantum leaps can one person take in a lifetime without learning that infinity exists only in some other universe, a different element of the physical world? Why did Jack send her this manuscript? Felicity asks herself, looking down at her toes. Is this what she feels? She marvels as she stands on her cliff of choice to ensure accomplishment.

"Temptation is the inclination of sin." Francis joins Felicity on the edge of the cliff, kicking dirt over the edge.

Felicity turns to see her cousin and grins, with head down.

"I thought I heard you arrive," says Francis, "but you didn't come in the house. Your footprints led me to you. When was the last time you were at Swallow's Edge?"

"I was just a little girl," Felicity recalls, and then she kisses Francis on both cheeks.

"It's nice to have you back with us. Mother is in the greenhouse." He gestures toward it.

Felicity takes Francis by the arm and puts her head on his shoulder. "How have you been?" she asks.

He wraps his arm around her, kissing her forehead. "I'm good. No, I'm great!"

They walk in silence before reaching the house.

"Lunch will be served soon. You hungry?" he asks while rubbing his stomach. "I'm starving!"

The crackling of the tiny pebbles beneath their feet follows them up to the house. The mansion appears smaller to Felicity than it used to be. The front garden, showcasing its autocratic style and dominating nature, bent to the will of man—or better yet, Aunt Hilda—stretches for a quarter of a mile to the front gates.

"I wasn't tempted to jump." Felicity brushes the leaves from the steps to take a seat. "How can you say temptation is a sin when—"

"Your doubt, your own reluctance, your fear," he quickly responds, standing before her with hands in the front pockets of his pants.

Elbows resting on the top step, she sits back. "I never know what you're talking about. How's the writing coming along? Your last play was a hit."

"She's not going to like you sitting there like that." Francis smirks. "Best we go in before she sends Norman after us. You remember Norman? I believe he's the oldest butler ever. I'm certain he's older than this house." Francis lifts Felicity off the step.

She stops him before they enter the house. "Will she be joining us for lunch?"

"She still believes you murdered your son. She hasn't gotten over that yet." Francis wraps his arm around her. "Never mind. She's loved you like her own daughter since you were born. She just can't understand how a mother could do what you did. She'll come around one day. Let's see how she is today. She may just have a sudden headache and ask that lunch be served to her in her room. That would be good for us. And yes, I'm writing. I just finished a short play for the kids in the village. They asked me to do something, and I wrote it last night. Still in draft if you're interested."

Felicity suddenly stops walking, eyes teary. "He begged and begged! Francis, does she not understand that? The moment Dr. Rees gave us the news, Luc made up his mind right there and then. I did everything I could to convince him otherwise. Do you know how difficult, how painful, how helpless it is for a mother to see her child suffer as he did? Luc's situation, his illness, progressed so quickly to the point where it was unbearable for him."

The room was warm, sterile, and filled with shelves of medical books. Luc and Felicity sat silently across the doctor's desk as she scanned the medical file. Luc grabbed a handful of jelly beans from a jar on the doctor's desk and stuffed them all in his mouth. Felicity's throat and lips were dry. She attempted to swallow to create saliva to moisten her mouth.

"We'll have to begin treatment tomorrow." The doctor closed the files. The loud silence pierced Felicity's head as she bent over and vomited on the floor.

"Mom, Mom." Luc bent down on his knees next to her to comfort her.

"Mrs. Moss, take this." Dr. Rees handed her a cloth and glass of water.

"Mom, it's OK. I knew it would be this. We both did." Luc sat back in his chair. "What are my chances, Doc?" He raised his hand, extending his index and middle finger. "One? Two?"

"One year, possibly two." The doctor returned to her desk, sat in her chair, and handed Luc a pile of medical pamphlets about chemotherapy treatments, the progressive symptoms of his cancer, and the eventual palliative care for which he must prepare.

"Hey, hey. It's OK." Francis hands her a handkerchief embroidered with "FM."

"Thank you. I'd love to read your play. What's the title?" Felicity wipes her eyes.

"*Desert Horse.*"

"What's it about?"

"Growing up."

"And what do you know about that?" she teases him as they enter the house.

Laughing, Francis shouts, "Mum, where are you? Felicity's here for the afternoon. I hope lunch is ready. We're starving!"

"You're terrible, Francis. She'll never come out now." She pokes him in the ribs.

"Let's eat. You remember how to find the dining room? I'll join you in a moment."

Felicity remembers the long hallways decorated with portraits of her ancestors. She arrives at the big solid-wood doors opening into an eighteenth-century-style dining room fit for kings. Aunt Hilda believes herself to be proper, well brought up, educated, and normal but does not see herself as the most eccentric character of the entire family.

"What's for lunch?" Francis asks, jogging to the table with manuscript in hand. "Here it is. It's the first time I've allowed myself to write something of such a nature. Have a read."

❖ ❖ ❖

Draft 1
Desert Horse

By
Francis Moss

CHARACTERS
Eden: A young boy
A **scorpion**

PLACE
Desert. Open space with dunes

TIME
Present day

SCENE I

Setting: Night after night, sleeping under desert stars, a boy notices a shape in the sky that he has never seen. One evening he decides to draw this shape in the hope that eventually he will know what it is. A scorpion appears.

SCORPION: What are you doing?

EDEN: I'm drawing that shape up there in the sky.

SCORPION: Why?

EDEN: Because I see it every night.

SCORPION: Why do you draw something you see every night?

EDEN: Because I'm hoping it will reveal itself to me.

SCORPION: Why do you need to know this?

EDEN: I don't know. I just feel I need to know.

SCORPION: There are many shapes in the sky. Why does this one interest you?

EDEN: In all my years, I have never seen this one before.

SCORPION: How could you say "in all my years" when you are just a boy?

EDEN: Should I not ask this what it is?

SCORPION: You can ask all the questions you want. But why ask a question to which you already know the answer?

EDEN: I know what this is?

SCORPION: Yes.

EDEN: I have seen this before?

SCORPION: Yes. (*Sits next to Eden.*) Do you remember what your mother said before you left on your journey?

EDEN: She told me always to remember my dreams so I would know where I am going and why.

SCORPION: So where are you going?

EDEN: That way. (*Points in the distance.*)

SCORPION: Who have you met while traveling this way?

EDEN: You.

SCORPION: No one else?

EDEN: I met a snake, but it continued on its way without talking to me.

SCORPION: Only one snake?

EDEN: No, a few, but they just kept going that way and that way (*Points in different directions.*) without visiting me.

SCORPION: And not once did any of them come talk to you?

EDEN: No, not once.

SCORPION: I wonder what you did to them to make them feel like they couldn't come to you.

EDEN: How do you know my mother said something to me before I left, and how do you know that I know the answer to my question?

SCORPION: You told me.

EDEN: How could I tell you something or give you an answer to something I don't even know the answers to myself?

SCORPION: It was a long time ago, Nathan, when we first met. You were the same age as you are now, in the same place, and going that way when you first told me all about your journey.

EDEN: My name is not Nathan. It's Eden. Why do you call me Nathan?

SCORPION: When I first met you, your name was Nathan.

EDEN: Where and when did we first meet?

SCORPION: We met where you are going.

EDEN: I don't even know where that is.

SCORPION: Yes, you do know where that is. You've been there before. It is where you lived and died.

EDEN: What do you mean it is where I lived and died? I'm here now and alive, so how could I have lived and died as well?

SCORPION: Before you were Eden, you were Nathan, a traveler on a pilgrimage for your life's purpose. When you reached the river, wild horses were running and playing, and you knew immediately that you were home. You found peace in this place because it felt right. You didn't go searching for why; you just knew it was right.

EDEN: Why did I want to come back again? If I told anyone about this or wrote about it, no one would believe me. They would think I spent too much time under the desert sun.

SCORPION: They might. Do you understand why you are here again, where you are going, why you are going that way again, and why the snakes have not stopped to spend time with you?

EDEN: No, no, no, and no. But it feels like I've heard this story before. I can't really explain why it's familiar to me.

SCORPION: Do you now know what the shape in the sky is?

EDEN: No.

SCORPION: It's a horse.

EDEN: A horse. Will I see one again? A real one?

SCORPION: That depends on you, Eden. You have chosen to return to this world because you wanted to return to them. However, this time, as last time, it is up to you if you wish to continue this journey or take a different road to explore what else you can see and learn.

EDEN: I don't really understand everything you say, but I understand what you are saying. I feel different now that I know all this. I feel I have been given a key to many doors, and I am free to choose whichever I want. What I feel the most is a desire to write, and the first thing I want to write about is these horses. I will call this book *Desert Horse*.

SCORPION: Do you now understand why the snakes that crossed your path did not stop to talk with you?

EDEN: No.

SCORPION: You were with these horses to look after them. You kept everything away that made them uneasy or nervous. As Eden, your subconscious remembered this—it remembered you as Nathan—and your thoughts sent out this energy that made the snakes feel uneasy around you, whether you intended to or not.

EDEN: I don't want them to fear me anymore. I want them to spend time with me and talk with me.

SCORPION: Now they will because you are aware of how strong your mind can be and how it can influence things around you for better or worse. You must remain aware of your consciousness and your ability to be the power that you are.

After sitting for quite some time, Eden decides to stand, but when he does, he feels different. The scorpion seems smaller and farther away than when he first appeared in the sand. When the sun begins to set, Eden notices that his shadow is longer than it was earlier that day. He looks down at his feet and realizes they aren't the feet he had earlier that day. They are much too big. Eden looks at his hands, and he falls over in the sand. He is terrified.

He doesn't know what is happening to him. He looks over at his friend, the scorpion, with tears in his eyes.

EDEN: What happened to me?

SCORPION: You grew old.

EDEN: I'm just a boy. How could I have grown to be an old man in just a few hours?

SCORPION: We haven't been here for just a few hours. We have been here for more than seventy years.

EDEN: That's a whole lifetime. How could I have been here, sitting in the same place, for more than seventy years? What happened to my life?

SCORPION: You lived it.

EDEN: How could I have lived an entire life and still be in the same place?

SCORPION: My friend, you have lived an entire life. When I first met you, you were on a journey headed that way. Then you learned something about yourself. There were many other moments of discovery. You arrived at where you were headed, fell in love, married, and had children and then grandchildren. Today you are where you have been seeking to be all this time. You are in the moment of reflection. This place today exists only in your memory. You sit here looking up at the sky, one of the most peaceful places you've ever been, where you began to see yourself and, most important, know yourself. For some, this moment of reflection occurs early in life or moments before they leave the bodies they are given. It is different for everyone. For you, my friend, it is now, when you are an old man. It's really that simple, so do not go searching for complex or mysterious answers to all your many questions. The boy I knew is still in you.

EDEN: Did I ever write my book, *Desert Horse*?

SCORPION: No, but you will, because now you know the entire story.

❖ ❖ ❖

They devour Aunt Hilda's traditional four-course lunch with a couple of bottles of red wine, followed by a few cognacs in the once men-only smoking room. Amy Winehouse is playing in the background. The house staff, unaccustomed to laughter and singing, remains perplexed, troubled, and unsure how to serve.

Felicity stretches out onto the long ruby red velvet covered sofa, kicks off her shoes and rest her head on the pillow. Her feet sink into the cold mud, moving back and forth, letting the black wetness climb up through her toes. The air is moist and cool. She gazes at the lichen hanging from the cathedral of trees—Douglas fir, western red cedar, hemlock, and grand fir—standing meters above her head. The stream rushes behind her. Tying her robe around her waist, she pulls herself out of the mud and rests on the emerald moss bed. The earthy, fresh, seductive odor keeps her lying there. Surrounded by lush layers of salal, huckleberry, Oregon grape, and sword fern, she reaches up to touch the full, bright moon. She must continue. She gets up and walks strong, listening to the night calls. Her stomach rumbles with hunger. She immediately detects and follows a rancid aroma. There it lays, rib cage exposed, tongue hanging out, guts spilled. She kneels next to it. She moves her hand up and down the warm corpse. She gently reaches in, moving her hand, searching. The tips of her fingers touch the warmth of a recently beating heart. Wrapping her hand around it, she rips it out of the deer's chest.

Felicity sits up and looks around the room to see Francis stretched out on another sofa. She looks at the clock above the fireplace: 8:00 p.m.

"Looks like you had quite a dream," says Francis, smiling.

"Jack sent me this manuscript. It's doing my head in."

"Are you going to do it?"

"Not sure yet. I don't know. We'll see." She gets up from the sofa, feeling and looking fuzzy. "I haven't done this in a while. Not since Luc died. And I've not seen Jack either since the trial. It's been seven years. I'm not sure if…"

"You might as well spend the night. It's late." Francis fully stretches, releasing a loud, explosive yawn. "Did you see what you wanted, and did you get done what you needed to do today?"

"Yes, thank you." Felicity looks up at Luc's portrait. She hears a creaking floorboard behind the smoking-room door as a shadow moves in and out. The light flickers in the crack between the door and the wooden floor. The butler's ear rests against the door, listening, but he doesn't dare enter.

3

Aromatic, gamy moose sausages sizzling on the stove; savory-sweet baked beans mixed with luscious, viscous maple syrup; and the rhythm of grinding freshly roasted coffee beans are the morning ritual in the Warthog household. This, along with the alpacas, with their wet, cool noses pressed against the kitchen window, unable to resist the heady redolence, is the highlight of Eliot's morning. Hearing the alpacas' heavy breathing and seeing their puffs of exhaled breath with lips curled, Eliot, a film director, recites his daily incantation: "I am life, I am laughter, I am love."

"And they say you are not beautiful," he says to the alpaca as if they can hear and understand. He presses his face against the window in a kissing motion.

Eliot takes the pan from the stove and scrapes the sausages onto his plate, along with a large scoop of beans, and he pours an added layer of oaky maple syrup over it all. The percolating coffee announces it is ready for Eliot to pour it into his favorite cup, handmade by his wife, Margaret, in one of her ceramic classes. Eliot and Margaret met during an audition that Eliot was directing. Margaret had tried out for the lead role of a male ballroom-dancing instructor. At the time, she was George Smith. George and Eliot dated for a number of years, George made the transition, and the wedding vows followed. Twenty years later, with the alpaca hobby farm, the Warthog name had become known throughout the township and loved by most. It's a friendly community, full of curious folks, some expressing their objections through whispers and stares.

Tap, tap, tap at the window. An alpaca rubs its head against the glass, calling for Eliot to come outside. He looks to see which of his ladies is calling to him. Henrietta's long eyelashes are Eliot's favorite feature.

"I'll be right there, my love," he promises as he shovels his breakfast into this mouth.

Margaret recently arrived home from a late-night shoot and went straight to bed. Eliot prepares her a breakfast tray with a rose and a little love note doodled on a breakfast napkin: "Live, laugh, love."

Eliot prepares for his daily walk into the small bayside town, Deep Cove, to get a taste of the fresh homemade doughnuts at the local family-owned restaurant. The Cove, as residents call it, is home to a forest, mountains, and an ocean; it is located at the foot of Mount Seymour. The Cove became a popular vacation area for Vancouver residents in 1910. Eliot's grandparents had fallen in love with it and purchased the home in which Eliot now resides.

The sheltered, calm harbor of the Cove is where Eliot and Margaret enjoy going kayaking, canoeing, and sailing when neither of them is working and they can spend their days together. Meandering down the hilly streets to the town's main drive, Eliot wonders if gray-haired, pipe-smoking Harold will be sitting on his favorite bench this morning.

Of course he will, Eliot muses. *And Mrs. Rouge will be taking her daily walk with her two Chihuahuas in tow.*

The usual characters are on the scene as Eliot makes his way to his favorite fast-paced, crowded restaurant. A string of tiny brass bells chimes as the door opens, and with it the smell of freshly cooked doughnuts fills Eliot's olfactory senses. He responds like one of Pavlov's dogs.

"Good morning, Warthog," says Clare, the restaurant's owner, as she hands him a doughnut and coffee on a tray.

"Good morning, Clare. Mrs. Rouge is on her way. She's just turned the corner. She should be about half an hour." Eliot snickers. He searches deep in his pants pocket for coins to pay Clare. He pulls out a handful of dimes, quarters, and loonies covered in lint. Picking out the bits, he places his hand on the counter next to the cash register, letting the coins roll off.

"How's Margaret doing today?" asks Clare, preparing a doggie bag for her.

"She's resting, Long night on the set. Better make it two, one of them chocolate. Luckily, this one is close to home. She's home every night."

"How are the kids doing? I hear one is off to Africa, working with animals?"

"Yes. That's Georgette. She's volunteering for a year. She's looking more and more like her mother these days."

They both giggle. Eliot takes his tray and sits at a small table in the corner, facing the cove.

Clare pours herself a cup of coffee and joins Eliot. "Tell me about this new film you're going to be working on," she says, adding a bit of sugar to her coffee.

"Ah…you know, this and that. Life. Stuff. I can't say the usual, though. This one is a bit perplexing." He bites into his doughnut and chews like an alpaca.

"I'm intrigued. Tell me more," she insists, sitting back in her chair as though indicating that she's settling in to hear the entire story.

"I haven't read the manuscript yet, just a summary. It's coming by DHL courier today. Should be there by the time I get back home. It's based on a short story. I read the book many moons ago."

"What's the title of the book?"

"*Write between the Lines*," he says and then sips his coffee. "You know it?"

"Yeah, I think I've heard of that book. Came out in the eighties. Yeah, I remember reading it. I didn't understand it much. It's like a mini version of *Ulysses*, by James Joyce. I remember reading the same lines over and over again to follow the story. The author is…What was her name? Ah, it will come to me."

"Viviane Shoemaker is the author," says Eliot, pulling the paperback book from his back pocket.

"Let me have a look." Clare opens the book and flicks the pages. "Yes, I remember now. I kept it in my bag for months because I was determined to get through it. It was one of my course assignments for English literature. She wrote this book when she was in her eighties. I recall reading that she had just celebrated her fourteenth birthday when the war broke out. She talks about generals and officials coming to her house and sitting for hours behind closed doors with her father. Later, in that same room, Hitler spent hours with her husband. He then ordered the killing of her husband. Then the men who killed her husband all died mysterious deaths. It was spring. Tulips were delivered to the families with no cards, no names—just 'Anonymous.' I believe they may have underestimated her. But I also recall reading that after her husband's death, she fell into a deep depression due to the shock of receiving his ashes in a wooden box. That was when *Writing between the Lines* was conceived, I presume."

"Margaret has a lover," Eliot blurts out, taking the book from Clare.

"No, she doesn't," Clare says with a laugh. "It's that wild imagination of yours. You always think that when she's working. What's wrong with you? She's just very engaging, let's say. People like being with her, being around her. George was like that with the women. She's not going to change. Besides, you have Henrietta."

Eliot chokes on his last sip of coffee, laughing. "I must make my way back home." He gets up and kisses Clare on the forehead.

"Eliot, give me a hand."

He turns to see Mrs. Rouge.

"Good morning, Mrs. Rouge. Lovely morning," he says and begins his stroll back home. He has a few stops to make on the way.

Clare runs out before he disappears from sight. "Are you going to the funeral this morning?"

"It's on the way home, so I might as well stop in. It's what's expected."

"Give this to Harold when you see him." Clare hands him a doggie bag filled with warm doughnuts and coffee. "These will last a few days.

He's been sitting there longer than usual, almost like he's waiting for something."

"Sure. I'll see what's going on with the old guy." Eliot takes the bag. He can see Harold in the distance, sitting on his own, watching the sea on a park bench facing the cove. Harold looks straight ahead, never looking left or right, never distracted by any of the kids playing around him. He has been sitting on this bench for the past twenty years, since his retirement. He and his wife were schoolteachers, loved by all. They retired on the same day and had great plans to travel the world. As young sixty-fivers, they had prepared their backpacks for a hike through Machu Picchu and a spectacular twenty-day boat trip to Antarctica on a small private yacht rigged up for explorers.

The locals in the community had organized an elaborate retirement and going-away beach party for the couple. The decorations reflected the journey they were about to embark on for the next three years. Flags of every nation they were to visit had been embedded in the sand in the shape of a circle, and maps were spread along the tables. After the party, Harold and his wife drove home. While they were listening to music and talking about their trip, their car was suddenly struck by an oncoming car. Harold walked away without a scratch. His wife was killed instantly; her head collided with the windshield despite her religious penchant for wearing her seat belt. She required a closed casket.

"Coffee and doughnuts from the lovely Clare." Eliot hands Harold the bag.

He takes it, opens it, brings it to his face, and inhales the smell of fresh doughnuts and coffee. Reaching into the bag, he pulls the coffee out, removes the lid, and takes a sip. Then he pulls a doughnut out and takes a big bite.

"It's a lovely day today," says Eliot. "You must come see Henrietta. She'll be excited to see you. You haven't been around for a while."

Harold takes another sip of coffee and then finishes all the doughnuts in the bag.

"I think some of those were meant for later," Eliot jokes, pointing at the bag.

Harold licks his lips and smiles.

"I'm curious, Harold. What's so intriguing out there today?"

"The body."

"What body?" says Eliot, clearly confused.

"The one that's coming," responds Harold.

"From where?" Eliot wonders, turning his head toward the water to see what Harold's looking at. "Are you waiting on a delivery from a mermaid?"

"Don't be silly. There's no such thing as mermaids." Harold looks at Eliot like he's an idiot.

"Yes, that's true. Silly me," Eliot says sarcastically.

Harold wipes his hands and places the empty coffee cup and folded bag next to him on the bench. "The body's going to come from around the bend, over there. You know the drowning that occurred a few days ago near Devil's Chin? They haven't found the body yet, and looking at the current, I believe it should be here."

"So you think the body will drift all the way from Devil's Chin to the Cove, Harold? I—"

"Are you questioning me?" Harold keeps looking forward.

"No, I just don't think—"

"I could hear those church bells all morning," Harold interrupts, changing the subject. He crosses his arms and legs.

"Yes, it's Ryan Cross's funeral today. I'll be heading up there on my way home later."

Ryan was a friend of Eliot's. He was also the one who had killed Harold's wife in the car accident.

"Catholic funerals…they're always so long. I guess it's the same when you've been murdered. It starts with the introductory rites. The family begins the greeting by sprinkling with holy water, and then there's the placing of the pall and whatever Christian symbol they want. The group chant, the opening hymn, and then the opening prayer. A reading from the book of Jacob, chapters nineteen to twenty-three: 'Then Jacob answered…'"

"Yes, it can go on and on and on," Eliot agrees. "Liturgy of the Word, of the Eucharist, and then the final commendation, which is why I have time."

"Ryan didn't have much luck on this earth. I hope he has better luck up there." Harold uncrosses his arms and legs. "I heard how they delivered his body to his mother, all the way from Florida. What was he doing in Florida anyway? I would have killed him myself at one time," he admits.

"You forgave him. That's why you didn't kill him yourself."

"Didn't do him any good. Look how he ended up."

"He could never forgive himself. He believed he could change himself, like he was told."

Eliot reaches into his back pocket for his wallet. The leather is worn and torn but held together by solid stitching. From inside one of the folds, he pulls out a tiny black-and-white photo of him and Ryan.

Eliot joined the Big Brothers association to help young men growing up without fathers or male role models. Unconventional as it was at the time, Eliot semiadopted Ryan because his mother could not accept that she had a gay son. Ryan was a handsome young man. The girls loved him. The boys hated him. The girls flirted with him, believing they could seduce him into changing. Ryan was also the star athlete of his high school. But under this overwhelming popularity, polarized with equal hatred, he got his head kicked in by the bullies one day, blinding him in his left eye. He managed to escape his tormentors. He struggled to remain conscious so he could drive himself to the hospital. Defeated and on the verge of passing out, he smashed into Harold's car on the way. He went in and out of drug rehabilitation for years after that. He managed to get into college to study theater. Many people recognized his talent as an actor. He was a success only because of his hard work and dedication. He was known as a chameleon. But he was still haunted; drugs followed him, and so did his attempt to change to a heterosexual man.

"That was when he was sixteen. He had just won a race," Eliot tells Harold as he holds up the photo. Harold takes it.

"Harold, Ryan was found hanging in a tree in Florida because of a drug deal gone bad. Well, that's what the cops say. He met a woman in Montreal and decided to follow her to Florida. That night, at a party, she reported he got into an argument and left without telling her or anyone else. The next morning, he was found hanging. The cops said it was suicide. But that made no sense because his clothes were ripped, and he had cuts on his body. His father's ring was missing, and so were a few of his other valuable belongings.

"The cops chose not to pursue it further. It was an obvious hate crime that will never be solved because the cops did not give a shit. They cremated his body without his mother's consent and informed her that they were sending her his belongings. When the package arrived, she opened a box that she believed contained a bag of sand because that's what it looked like at a quick glance. Knowing that Ryan had been in Florida, she thought he had collected sand to bring back home because she knew how much he loved the beach. When she placed her hand in the sand, she didn't understand why there were tiny sharp bits. She first thought they were broken-up shells, but then she looked closer. There, sprinkled in the palm of her hand, were her son's bones. The box was never labeled."

"He was a handsome chap." Harold hands the photo back to Eliot.

"I hope the mermaid delivers the body soon; otherwise, you'll be sitting here forever," teases Eliot.

Harold smirks.

❖ ❖ ❖

With a bit of time to kill before the funeral service at St. Martin's Church up on the hill, Eliot strolls along the boardwalk by the sea, stroking his chin, thinking he'll stop in for a much-needed shave at Shuffle & Son's barber shop, family owned since 1896. The place had not changed much since then, with the exception of general upkeep and upgrades of the electrical and plumbing systems. A couple of times a week, Eliot sits in the raised wooden chair from 1896—with new seat padding, of course—and contemplates life while being buffed and patted. Arched far enough in the chair, with the blade sliding across his throat in swift, gentle strokes, his mind focused on the patterns above him on the ceiling, counting every tiny flower.

Who or what is Margaret thinking of when she talks about the alpacas, the manuscript? Eliot wonders, tripping on a tiny crack. The tide is very high this morning; waves crash into the wall, splashing him as he walks. The hypnotic thrashing makes his mind wander even more.

Distracted by a seal swimming quickly in and out of the water, Eliot stops. The seal has caught a salmon. Eliot can see the seal bobbing vertically in the water, its head in clear sight, holding on to a salmon almost as big as it is. It's as though the seal is showcasing his catch. Everyone on the boardwalk stops to watch in amazement.

Stepping off the boardwalk and onto the grass to cross the street, Eliot sees Mr. Shuffle sitting out in front of his shop with a cup of tea. As he notices Eliot, he lifts his hand to wave hello.

"Good morning, Eliot," says Mr. Shuffle. "How's Harold today? Tell him to come in for a shave. He's not been around for a couple weeks."

"Will do. Good morning to you too." Eliot rubs his chin. He helps Mr. Shuffle from his chair, opens the shop door, and walks in. Mr. Shuffle is the oldest barber in the entire area. With a steady hand and full of stamina, the eighty-two-year-old historical member of the community has been working in the family shop since he was old enough to sweep the floor. He refuses to retire. The day he'll retire is when he'll come close to drawing blood, and that day has not happened yet.

Eliot sits in his usual chair, greeting himself in the mirror, and reclines in a submissive position, an animal exposing his belly. Thirty minutes later he stops staring at the ceiling. He is clean-shaven. Mr. Shuffle puts him back in the normal seated position and slaps a bit of tonic on his cheeks.

"Good as new," says Mr. Shuffle. "You on your way—"

"Yes." Eliot cuts him off. The clock hanging on the wall behind him indicates that he is running late. "Thank you. See you next week."

Eliot strokes his smooth, shaven face as he walks up the hill, taking the long way to get to the church. When he reaches the street corner, he can see people walking out of the church, getting into vehicles. The funeral mass is over; he is too late. He stands there, watching the cotillion of people, all dressed in black, greeting one another with polite gestures, hats raised, wearing dark glasses, sniffling into tissues. The boys who blinded Ryan are also there. They had served fifteen-year sentences for their crime. Ryan had no choice but to forgive them when they repented. As grown men, realizing what ugliness they had embraced at one time in their lives, they were truly remorseful for their actions.

All the faces are familiar, even those unexpected to attend. Eliot walks toward the cars, waiting to decide which one he will enter. Mrs. Cross embraces Ryan's urn as though she were reliving holding him as a newborn. She disappears into the first limo. Eliot walks toward the last car, opens the door, and slides in quietly. The driver nods. A few seconds later, the other passenger door opens. A man steps into the car and sits next to Eliot. Surprised, the man looks over at him.

"Hi," says Eliot.

"You missed the mass," says Jack as he settles in. "I thought I saw Alfred motioning down the street."

"I think he's with Felicity." Eliot puts on his seat belt.

"He's keeping her there. I need her back on set."

"She's keeping herself there," says Eliot.

"Luc was also my son." Jack looks out the window to see if everyone has gotten into their cars.

"He didn't know that. You contributed to her need in the privacy of a doctor's office with a titty magazine and a plastic jar, and thank goodness he had her looks." Eliot presses the button to roll down the window for some air. The procession of cars begins moving.

❖ ❖ ❖

Felicity helped herself to a cognac while waiting for Jack to return to his office. "How was the session?" she asked as he walked through the door.

"When will you come with me?" Jack poured himself a drink.

"I can't be doing that right now. I need to spend most of my time with Luc." Felicity took a seat at the end of the sofa, below the Oscar Wilde portrait.

"The support groups are very helpful. He's my son, and I need to know how to deal with this." He sat next to her and put his feet up on the coffee table. He reached for a cigar in the cigar bar on the table next to Felicity. "Do you mind?"

"Yes." She took a sip of her cognac. "I never liked those cigars. Why don't you quit?" She turned to him. Jack threw the cigar onto the table. He covered his face with his hands, releasing a huge sigh. Felicity put her arm around him. "I know it's difficult, Jack. I know how much you love him."

Jack rested his head back on her arm. "Does he still want to call it quits this week?"

"Yes. But I keep all the meds and hide anything I think he can kill himself with. He hates me for this. Some days he does everything he possibly can to hurt me, to try to get me to hate him, to be sick of him and his belligerent behavior so I agree to kill him right there and then. He sometimes, even on the good days when he can make his own way to the bathroom, will purposely piss and shit his pants and watch me clean it up."

Jack got up off the couch to get the bottle of cognac from the bar. "I don't know how you do it every day, Felicity. You're stronger than I am. I probably would have obliged him months ago. He is now over his one-year mark. I believe he's now on borrowed time." He topped off her glass.

"No, the doctor said one year, at best two. So why take that chance away from him?" She kicked off her shoes and stretched out on the sofa. Jack stared at Oscar Wilde. "He's persistent; I have to give him that much. He's so determined to die. He's never wanted to get treatment, any. I had to convince him for my sake to at least start something, with the meds and then chemo." Tears rolled down her face as she wept silently.

"Felicity, please. I hate to see you like this. You're breaking my heart. Had I said no when you asked me to be the donor, you would not be suffering like this now." Jack sat at his desk chair. "I know it's a stupid thing to say. I feel totally fucking helpless. You were always determined to have this child on your own. I agreed with it then. Now I'm not so sure it's right anymore for me to remain anonymous."

Felicity sat up and emptied her glass. "Jack, I wanted a child so much, and I'm grateful for you. I could only do this on my own. You know me—I'm not someone who can be in a relationship just for the sake of being in one. I could never have someone in my life who wasn't right for me. Now I have Alfred. If only I had met him then; it would have been lovely to have children with him. The clock was ticking, as they say, and you were my first choice. You've been a great friend to Luc his entire life. You were there for all of his birthdays, school plays, piano lessons, and performances. He has your hands and plays the piano just like you. He's even just a bit better than you, our little child prodigy. He's had a wonderful life, Jack, because he's been loved and knows how to love. He was raised to be the kind of man that women love because he's kind and authentic. Chivalry is something he's learned from the get-go. Women still love that, by the way. You mean the world to him, Jack."

❖ ❖ ❖

"When do you think Ryan will let us know he's crossed over?" asks Jack.

"Not sure. It's not like he can just pick up the phone." Eliot continues looking out the window at the autumn colors, as though God himself has just taken time out of his busy schedule, on this day, to paint the leaves the brightest oranges, reds, and yellows that Eliot has ever seen.

Eliot has this thing, this sixth sense with which to see the dead, that he's had ever since he was a little boy. They would visit him, sometimes shortly after they died, or sometimes years later. The troubled souls would seek him out, as did Bob. While he had been shooting a film in Vancouver, Eliot decided to stay in a quaint little bed-and-breakfast instead of his regular big, fancy hotel. One night, while in bed, he was woken up by an odd feeling. He looked at the clock: 3:00 a.m. This went on for about three weeks. Each time he woke up, he would see a figure standing over his bed, looking down at him. He was never frightened. He could feel a curious yet lonely and distressed energy.

One night he called out the name "Bob." He wasn't quite sure what Bob wanted, but he knew Bob had been stuck for years and needed help moving on. The energy in the room was getting stronger and stronger, draining Eliot of his energy. He couldn't get enough sleep, and he was beginning to feel unwell. Eliot told Bob that he could come and speak to him any time during the day and asked that he please stop waking him up in the middle of the night.

Eliot wanted to find out if anyone else in the building had felt Bob's energy. He asked the B and B owner if he had ever felt anything or seen anything. The owner had, but didn't know what it was. He told Eliot a story about a couple who had stayed in the same room. The wife kept asking her husband why he kept moving certain things or hiding them. He didn't know what she was talking about. This went on the entire time they stayed at the B and B until they realized that someone or something was in the room with them.

The room was furnished with beautiful antiques. When Eliot moved in, he noticed a book that had been left behind on the table. Its title was something like *Life after Death* or *We Never Really Die*. He didn't make much of it at the time, but then he realized that Bob had been an unwanted guest for some time. Eliot needed to do something. He decided to do some research on the place and its original owners. The house had been built in 1753. Eliot discovered that before it had been remodeled into a beautiful B and B by a very wealthy family known to be members of a group that held frequent séances, a young man named Bob had lived and died in that very same house. He had been found dead next to where Eliot slept.

Eliot needed to help Bob cross over, and he needed to do it soon because his own health was deteriorating due to lack of sleep. He went to the local spiritual store to purchase white sage to smudge in the bedroom and to encourage Bob to cross over. The smoke from the burning sage cleared the space of unwanted energy, leaving it purified.

Eliot also smudged around his body and objects in the room to clear the energy.

After the smudging, Eliot planned to stay in another room to let the spirit move on. While he prepared his overnight bag to move to the new room, he talked to Bob, telling him what he was doing and why. The energy Eliot felt was like that of a two-year-old boy having a tantrum. Bob did not want Eliot to leave, and he didn't know where Eliot was going.

When Eliot burned the sage next to his bed, he felt Bob tugging at his shirt. He could see and feel this movement. It was like the trick where a magician raised a handkerchief without touching it. All Eliot could see was the fabric moving. Eliot was scared, and he did not understand what was happening. He felt that Bob had become too attached to him. He was a safe place for Bob, but Eliot knew that this was not the best place for Bob. Eliot wanted him to be at peace and move on with his life—yes, it was a life, and he needed to continue it.

While this was happening, Eliot looked down at the smoke coming from the burning sage. The smoke went straight up and then, at about a foot from the base of the sage, flowed directly at a ninety-degree angle along the length of the bed.

Eliot did his best to console Bob, but he needed more help. Suddenly, he felt his cousin and his grandfather in the room. He knew they were there to help him with Bob's crossing. Eliot couldn't have asked for anyone better, because both his cousin and his grandfather knew firsthand the pain and suffering that came from drugs and alcohol. He continued burning the sage and talking to Bob, his grandfather, and his cousin. After he finished what he had to do, he left the room, not knowing if any of this was going to be successful. But as he was walking away, his gut feeling told him that Bob had begun to move toward the light and that he was going to be OK.

Eliot slept well that night in the other room. The next morning, he returned to his original room, and when he opened the door, he felt a lightness he had not experienced there since he'd first arrived. He felt that Bob had moved on. Now Bob could begin to heal and continue on with his life. And Eliot could, thankfully, catch up on some much-needed sleep.

The manuscript, never far from anyone's mind, is rolled up tightly in Jack's inside coat pocket. The procession of cars nears the house. One by one, people exit their vehicles and walk toward Mrs. Cross's mansion on the hill, disappearing behind the large, wooden doors, a local carpenter's masterpiece. On them, the story of Jesus from birth to his crucifixion is illustrated in the finest carvings imaginable.

"Do you sleep with it as well?" Eliot points to the manuscript sticking out of Jack's pocket.

"If I must," replies Jack as if it were a completely natural thing to do so.

They both remain in the car.

"Felicity knows you're here," says Eliot. "You have to go into the house."

"You're coming with me," instructs Jack.

"Are you sure she's up for this?" asks Eliot, pulling the manuscript out of Jack's pocket.

"Don't be such a faggot, and just fuckin' get her back on set!" demands Jack, snatching the manuscript back. "I don't know why you insist on dragging this out."

"I'm the faggot? You're the faggot, and you're an idiot. I'm not the one who thinks he's lived a past life with good old Oscar Wilde. He was never your lover, and I don't think you've come to accept that reality."

"Reality? Oh, that's rich coming from someone who names all of his alpacas. Henrietta? Yes, Henrietta is an alpaca. She's not your second wife!" Jack explodes as he unfastens his seat belt. "Warthog, we need to make an appearance. Now let's go. I want you to come with me. I know he was like a son to you." As if to lighten the mood, he changes the focus. "*Warthog.*" He exaggerates the name. "I could never get used to that. Why didn't your folks ever change their name?"

"Harold's waiting for the mermaid to drift to shore," Eliot declares, still strapped in and showing no sign that he's ready to get out of the car. "Alfred went looking for the body. He and Samuel were at the beach house when the siren went off at Devil's Chin."

"I hear she was quite the mermaid. Expensive, but worth every penny. They say she jumped." Jack leans over to unlock Eliot's seat belt.

"She didn't jump. She was pushed," Eliot explains as he slides the seat belt from his shoulder. "Like moths to a flame, all men wanted her—some more than others, and one could not, evidently, let her go. It makes for a good story. *The Tragedy of the Moth.* The murderer has been arrested. She was known as Madame Bijou for the diamond tattoo on her buttocks."

Eliot opens the car door. "Let's do this," he says to Jack.

The sun's rays cast a glitter of crystals onto the sea, bright lights flickering into their eyes as they walk toward the house. Jack shades his with the manuscript.

"Put it away," says Eliot. Jack folds the manuscript back into his coat pocket.

As they reach the house, the front door opens. The butler welcomes them in and takes their coats. Most of the house is filled with people they've never seen before or known to be in Ryan's life. The mourners include Mrs. Cross's church group; the family priest, Father Martin Enders; and, to Eliot's and Jack's surprise, a longtime family friend, once known as Father Jacob, who now is accompanied by his wife.

Quite scandalous how he was allowed through the doors. Jack and Eliot thought the same thing at the same time, with a big "fuck off, who cares" smirk.

Father Jacob had been the church's head pastor for more than twenty-five years. Then one day, quite unexpectedly, he announced he was leaving. Amazed by this sudden admission, the parishioners quickly learned that Father Jacob and the church secretary had developed a very close friendship. After twenty years of this, Father Jacob requested a yearlong sabbatical from the parish to reevaluate his calling. His request was rejected. Not to be denied, Father Jacob left the church of his own accord and married his love.

Father Martin Enders, on the other hand, had been a schoolmate of Ryan's from kindergarten to high school. They had trained together as the top school athletes.

Eliot and Jack search the crowd for Mrs. Cross. The house is decorated with fine art and, at the far end of the spectrum, Christian statues. Eliot spots Mrs. Cross sitting in a corner, rocking her baby boy. As a waiter walks past, Eliot and Jack each grab a drink with both hands, down it, and place it back on the tray before the waiter is out of reach.

"Mrs. Cross, our deepest and most sincere condolences," Eliot says as he and Jack bend over, placing their hands on her shoulders. She looks up at them with a blank stare and then back down at the urn she holds gently in her arms. Behind her is a series of family photos. One of them jumps out at Jack and Eliot. It's a picture of Ryan dressed as a girl when he was five years old.

"Well, there you go," says Jack. "Get us a drink." He gestures with his head to Eliot, who motions to the waiter and grabs more drinks from the tray.

"Check this place out," says Eliot. "A mix between the Vatican, the Louvre, and art deco. What era are we in? What's with the orange walls? Too much money to make too much of a mess. I know it's a funeral, but come on. Can it be any more depressing? Look at these people. This is not what Ryan would have wanted."

Jack downs his drink. They continue scanning the room, looking at the holier-than-thou icons along the wall and their followers nursing their drinks. And just like that, out of nowhere, they both begin laughing hysterically, out of control. Placing their hands to their mouths, trying not to disturb the somber mood, they make their way to the garden doors and head outside.

4

"Interesting title. Interesting idea," Eliot muses as he reads 'Tulip' at the top of the first page of the script. Before he turns the page, he notices a letter in the DHL courier envelope addressed to him at Warthog Productions.

Dear Warthog,

For Warthog Productions's consideration:

The students have worked together to create this short film. They are writers and actors, not directors or producers yet. You are invited to join the youth group in the realization of their first short film. We appreciate your demanding schedule, the alpacas you care for, and the community you serve. Nonetheless, we expect that you will accept our invitation to join us.

Your loving friend,
Felicity
PS: Soon.

Tulip

By
Sabrina Wright
Arnold Winters

CHARACTERS
Ben: Husband of Caroline; ex-husband of Joyce; has a brain tumor and fewer than six months to live; poor motor skills; left side of his body is weaker and drags
Caroline: Wife of Ben
Joyce: Ex-wife of Ben; surrogate mother of Ben and Caroline's baby; seven months pregnant
Teferi: Aid to Ben

PLACE
Ben and Caroline's house

TIME
Present day

SCENE I
KITCHEN TABLE—MIDDAY

TEFERI, a young African American, is sitting at the kitchen table, peeling apples with little stickers on each one displaying the word organic. BEN, a once-robust young man, now weak, is sipping tea at the table, looking out the window. Medicine bottles are scattered across the table. A prepared lunch (soup heating on the stove, sandwiches on the counter, covered with a light cloth) is waiting to be eaten.

TEFERI: I found these apples you like. They are bloody expensive. You sure you don't want to eat the apple peel? I might as well throw out half the money you give me if you don't want to eat the whole apple.

Ben gets up from the table, walks to the fridge, opens the door (organic food stacked inside), and takes out two beers. He fumbles for a bottle opener in a nearby drawer and drops it. Teferi goes to get up and get the opener for him, but Ben signals with his hand for him to stay where he is. Ben manages to pick up the bottle opener; he walks to the table, opens the beers in a clumsy manner, and sets one in front of Teferi. Ben drinks his beer.

TEFERI: (*Staring at Ben.*) You know you're not supposed to have alcohol right after you take your meds. You're supposed to wait at least an hour. Better yet, don't even touch the stuff.

Ben takes a big gulp of beer and lets out a ferocious burp. Teferi tries not to laugh.

TEFERI: (*Smiling eyes.*) You know, if they catch us, it's my head!

BEN: I wish.

Teferi looks at Ben with disappointment.

❖ ❖ ❖

The office door slams. Eliot, irritated, doesn't need to look up to see who's arrived. It's Dumas, Chester Dumas, his production manager.

"Don't let that door slam," says Eliot.

"Fix it," replies Dumas. He notices the manuscript. "More work, I see. I signed for it last night. I see it's from her. Is she coming back?"

"Her students," Eliot explains.

Chester pours coffee beans into the grinder, prepares his favorite cup, and cleans Eliot's cup. Water boils for the coffee press. Tall, handsome Chester stands over Eliot's shoulder.

"Does it have potential?" Chester asks.

"Just started. Don't know yet. We'll see," Eliot says, shrugging to get Chester out of his face.

Chester opens the office windows to let in some fresh air. "I don't know why you insist on keeping these closed when you're working. The sea is right in front of you. The fresh air will clear your brain, Warthog."

He hands Eliot his cup of coffee. Eliot takes three short but loud sips to avoid burning his lips and goes back to reading the manuscript.

❖ ❖ ❖

BEN: I'm sorry.

The sound of a key in the front door startles them. They down their beers, and then Teferi grabs the bottles and hides them in his bag. Ben takes one of the peeled apples and starts to eat it. Teferi continues to peel the apples.

TEFERI: Once she's settled in, I'll make apple pie. It's her favorite.

Ben and Teferi look at each other. Ben takes his walking stick and walks out of the kitchen.

SCENE II
LIVING ROOM—LATER, SAME DAY

BEN enters the living room, where CAROLINE and JOYCE have just dropped Joyce's bags and suitcases. Ben stands looking at both women, whom he loves dearly, sitting on the sofa. He blows a kiss to both of them. Caroline is helping Joyce with a pillow for her back.

BEN: Anything else to bring in?

CAROLINE: No. We have it all under control. Thank you, honey. Doesn't Joyce look great? We finally have her home with us.

Ben smiles at them both and walks toward them, tripping over nothing on the floor. He looks down at his feet to see what caused him to trip and then continues walking toward Caroline. He gives her one solid kiss on the lips. He then turns to Joyce and kisses her on the forehead and rubs her round belly.

BEN: How are we doing today? You're getting bigger by the minute.

JOYCE: Thanks! We are doing fine.

Joyce farts. They all laugh.

BEN: This calls for a drink. Teferi, come join us! It's good to have you home, Joyce. I'm glad you agreed to spend these last couple of months with us and have the baby here.

Joyce smiles at both Caroline and Ben but with a worried, pensive look in her eyes. Something is on her mind. Teferi walks into the living room.

❖ ❖ ❖

"Harold's mermaid drifted to shore this morning," Chester interrupts as he places a doughnut on top of the manuscript. Eliot takes the doughnut, wipes away the crumbs, takes a big bite, and continues reading.

❖ ❖ ❖

BEN: Here he is. He's been busy peeling apples. He's making your favorite, Joyce—all-organic apple pie!

Teferi greets both women and walks to the bar. He looks over at Caroline.

TEFERI: How are you both doing? The housework is done, and lunch is ready. Caroline, I made your favorite—organic tomato soup with tuna sandwiches with those little organic chives and sea salt. What are we drinking?

They all giggle.

CAROLINE: Awesome! Thank you. But Ben shouldn't have a drink. Remember, honey, what the doctor said? You can't mix alcohol with your meds. It will affect your motor skills, and they're already challenged. If you would have had a drink earlier, your tripping just now could have resulted in your falling flat on your face.

Teferi, keeping busy at the bar, moves bottles around to see what cocktails he can create. He keeps his head down, not making eye contact with either Ben or Caroline. He looks at Joyce, wondering what she's thinking about as she looks down at her belly.

BEN: Yes, honey…I wouldn't want to fall on my face. Pour us a drink, Teferi. Whiskey on the rocks for me. Joyce, what's your poison? Honey, white wine?

CAROLINE: Honey, you know Joyce can't drink right now. (*Looking at Teferi.*) Make her a virgin strawberry daiquiri. White wine for me. I bought a new organic Italian pinot grigio, top shelf.

Joyce gets up and walks to the bar to sit with Teferi. Ben sits with Caroline on the sofa.

❖ ❖ ❖

Drrrrrr…drrrrrr…drrrrrr…

Chester loves using the shredder for his monthly housekeeping. In a trance, he stands in front of the shredder, staring at each piece of paper as it gets chewed into the bin one page at a time.

"Eliot, Mrs. Rouge was at the coffee shop this morning. When I was waiting for my order, she looked up at me and said, with her red lips covered in doughnut crumbs, 'Hey, Dumas, I read in the papers just now that that woman…you know, the one who cut off her husband's penis years ago?' 'Lorena Bobbitt,' I say, to show interest and all that. 'Yes, that's her. Well, she moved to Eastern Europe.' 'Oh yeah,' I say, like I give even less of a shit. Then she goes on to say that Lorena Bobbitt changed her name, and I, of course, ask, 'To what?' 'Lorena Kuturcokoff.' Mrs. Rouge then burst into uncontrollable laughter. We all did. You have to admit, it's quite funny. I had to give her that at least."

Eliot bursts into laughter, and they both bend over in hysterics. They didn't know if they were laughing because the joke was funny or because it was Mrs. Rouge who had told such a joke.

❖ ❖ ❖

JOYCE: (*Taking her drink from Teferi.*) How's our boy doing today?

Joyce is eating snacks at the bar like it's been her only meal in days.

JOYCE: Is there any reason why Ben has stopped combing his hair and shaving? Stubble is sexy, though.

TEFERI: Yeah…I think he's sexy too. (*Speaking to Ben.*) Come here, sexy, and bring your wife her drink.

Ben stumbles to the bar and takes the glass of wine and then walks to Caroline, spilling some on the way. He hands her the glass and spills some on her as well.

BEN: Sorry, honey.

Caroline giggles in full acceptance. He sits next to her, cuddling her in his arm, which flops around her shoulder. Caroline smiles, illuminating her love for Ben. Joyce sips her virgin daiquiri. Her stillness echoes in the room. Teferi watches her, wondering what she's thinking about. He pours Ben a whiskey on the rocks and brings it to him.

TEFERI: (*With a smirk on his face.*) Here. On the rocks, as requested. Would you like anything else before I pour myself a drink?

BEN: No thanks.

Teferi heads back to the bar. He pours a white wine and sits down with Joyce.

TEFERI: So, Joyce, from the looks of that big belly, you're about to have this baby. How many more weeks?

JOYCE: Eight weeks. (*She sips her daiquiri.*) I came up with a name.

CAROLINE: For whom?

❖ ❖ ❖

Chester pulls up a chair next to Eliot.

"When's the next audition, or are we done?" he asks as he kicks Eliot's chair. "I've read the manuscript several times and made a few changes. I think you'll agree with me, as usual. What's everyone else think of this?"

"Not sure. We'll see," Eliot replies, looking up over his glasses, which are hanging off the tip of his nose.

"It'll no doubt be a hit, but you're going to cop a lot of shit for telling the story this way," Chester warns as he leans back in his chair, sipping his coffee.

"We'll see." Eliot pushes his glasses a bit higher and returns to the manuscript.

The last time Eliot worked on a film in which he added a great deal of his own changes was with Felicity. The film was in postproduction when Luc was in the hospital. Luc by then was in his supposedly final year of life. When Luc was in the hospital, Felicity spent all her time at the hospital as well, making it necessary for Eliot to have all their meetings in the hospital cafeteria. Luc was such a likable person that everyone just fell in love with him, making it difficult for everyone to see him suffer so much. Eliot and Margaret were very fond of Luc, and they visited him often.

"Is this another one of your award-winning films, Eliot?" Luc had asked in his weak and frail voice.

"Of course," Eliot had replied with a smirk, handing Luc his glass of water. They had both giggled.

❖ ❖ ❖

JOYCE: The baby.

TEFERI: I think it's time for lunch. Let's eat before Joyce eats the bar. I'll bring the bags up to her room. Ben, finish setting the table.

Caroline brings her glass to the bar. She gives Joyce a look. Joyce returns the look.

JOYCE: We talked about this. It's my body; I can name it. It's the only thing I asked, remember?

CAROLINE: Let's eat.

Teferi picks up the bags while the girls walk out, leaving Ben standing there.

SCENE III
JOYCE'S ROOM—LATER, SAME DAY

TEFERI is standing in JOYCE's room with her bags dropped next to him. He looks around. He places the bags on the bed, opens them, and takes out Joyce's clothes. He places them in drawers and hangs her dresses. Talking to himself, he finishes putting the clothes away. He then takes her perfume, brings it close to his nose, holds it there for a moment, taking in the scent, and places it on top of the dresser. He gently arranges the flowers that are there in a vase.

TEFERI: (*To himself.*) These people are crazy. How could they have thought this would ever work? What was Ben thinking? I can't figure out if he's hopeful, desperate, or a dreamer.

Joyce is standing in the doorway.

❖ ❖ ❖

"That's disgusting. Go take five minutes in the toilet, will you?" Eliot screeches at Chester.

"It's that bloody East Indian food I ate last night. Consequence: uncontrollable flatus via the anus, leaving a ring of fire. I wanted to see how hot I could take it!"

"Whatever," Eliot says as he looks at Chester in horror. "Go away!" He waves his arm, repulsed.

Chester moves to take the manuscript. "Will you let me read this one before you take it apart?"

"We'll see." Eliot pushes him away.

❖ ❖ ❖

JOYCE: (*Entering her bedroom.*) We are waiting for you. Lunch is on the table.

TEFERI: I'll be right down.

JOYCE: Ben's doing great! We're lucky to have you here. It's made such a difference to Ben that you've come back into our lives. He talked about you all the time. He would sit forever, telling stories of the two of you when you were boys. Your adventures—you were true explorers. He could not go on this adventure without you.

Joyce looks down at her round belly, touching it. Teferi sits on the edge of the bed.

JOYCE: I know you love him. Thanks for putting my things away. All that great food you made is getting cold. Let's go eat.

SCENE IV
KITCHEN TABLE—SAME DAY

CAROLINE, BEN, TEFERI, and JOYCE are sitting at the kitchen table. Lunch is laid out before them—an organic feast fit for a king. Joyce hands her plate to Ben. He fills it to the exact portions he knows she can eat. He hands her back the plate, looking her in the eyes with peace and joy. Joyce takes the plate from his wobbly hand.

BEN: Thank you.

Caroline takes Joyce's hand and kisses it.

JOYCE: OK, you guys, knock it off. If it's going to be like this every day, I'll go back home. Let me be! (*Beat.*) Teferi, how is your writing coming along? What are you writing about these days?

TEFERI: I've got writer's block—completely void of imagination for some time now. I think maybe I'll write about you crazy people. How's your husband, by the way? When will he be joining us?

JOYCE: He'll be back in time for the big day. They're shooting the last few weeks of the documentary they started a few years ago. You know him, he's been following lions his entire life. There you go! You can write about the adventures the three of you had when you were boys. And how one has become a world-renowned author who can take his readers on a journey of wonder and mystery intertwined with the good, the bad, and the ugly of what makes us human. And the other an amazing neurosurgeon. Ah, Dr. Ben, all the lives you saved. So, you see, there's plenty to write about. (*Beat.*) Caroline, how's your new CD coming along? I see you hit the top-ten country charts once again.

❖ ❖ ❖

The windows begin to rattle from the wind building up along the coastline. A storm is rolling in. The gray, dark sky's ghostly shadows paralyze the ability to relax. Suddenly, the wind crashes against the windows, forcing Eliot and Chester from their chairs. They quickly secure all the windows. At the door, Whiskers, the cat, is scratching to be let in. Chester is summoned by the loud *meow-meow-meow.* Immediately obeying the cry to be let in, he opens the door. Behind Whiskers, coming up the stairs, is Alfred.

"Well, look what the cat dragged in." Chester opens the door wider, welcoming Alfred.

"What a surprise! Alfred, come on in. Coffee?" asks Eliot as he takes a mug from the shelf and pours Alfred some coffee with a drop of milk.

With a sense of inquisitive uneasiness, they all sit and smile politely, all believing Alfred to be impervious to human emotion. Eliot offers him a doughnut.

"No, thank you," Alfred says politely, sipping his coffee and looking down at the manuscript.

"I see you received it. Not too bad for a bunch of kids—or should I say young adults, who decided to do this as their assignment over a long weekend instead of partying. Good piece of work for their first time." He points at the manuscript.

Eliot raises his cup of coffee to him in agreement. "Up to now, they've done all right."

Placidness and passiveness are not among Chester's traits. Avoiding all evasive behavior, he looks at Alfred straight on and says, "Now that you are wedged between us, tell us: how are things at the beach house?"

"It's like a strike of the match lately," replies Alfred.

"How do you mean?" asks Chester, perplexed.

"Samuel is with us. He's like a rash that never goes away."

They all laugh.

"Chaos." Alfred continues his rant. "No, madness. No, I don't think there's even a word to describe how it is when he's in your world. Felicity loves him. She has this ability to not let him get the better of her…I don't know how she does it." Alfred walks to the window. "Looks like I got here just in the nick of time. Samuel has this oratory ability to deliver words, ideas, philosophies, in a manner that traps you. He piques your curiosity to no end and then, just as suddenly, snaps you out of your trance by breaking his own pattern of wit that snared you in the first place. Most creatures of such a sort destroy their prey. Not him. He releases you, fracturing your foundation even more. How far are you into the manuscript?"

❖ ❖ ❖

CAROLINE: Teferi, I noticed some of your scribbles on my to-do notepad. You can't be all that void of imagination. What are you creating? The scribbling I read was "love, ride." What are you creating with such words?

TEFERI: I didn't write that. Must be someone else. (*Looks over at Ben.*) What have you been up to? What's going on in that head of yours?

BEN: Nothing!

Ben gets up from his chair. Even though he is clumsy, he dances around the table, reciting his poem.

La Vie en Rose

La vie en amour
Is a heart contained in amber,
Une vie vécu

Comment aimer
Plus qu'une fois,
Je vois cette femme
Someone to love

Where does love go
When something ends,
Une vie en rose
Like a flower it grows

Ben sits and continues eating his lunch. He picks up the little dish with his pills. Everyone is sitting there silently, watching him. Then they all start laughing.

❖ ❖ ❖

"When are you going to work with these kids?" asks Alfred. "This is better than some of the crap sent your way." He waves the manuscript in the air.

Eliot takes it from him. "It needs work. Why are you here, anyway?"

"Did you hear of the ebola outbreak in Guinea?" asks Alfred, changing the subject. "Rose is still there. She hasn't finished her documentary. The virus is no longer contained. It's out of control."

Eliot pours everyone another cup of coffee.

"She still has another six weeks before she's done," Alfred continues. "The wildlife documentary is scheduled to air early next year, and she's determined to stay on target. She never says much, just that all is OK and that they're taking precautionary measures."

"What does Jack say about all this?" asks Eliot as he hands the cups to Alfred and Chester.

"She's Jack's baby sister. He's sick with worry, of course. Rose has reported that some villages don't believe this disease is real. They believe that the medical teams are bringing on the disease to make money."

"What happened? How did it get to this point?" asks Chester, sucking on his pen.

"The first victim was a two-year-old child. It's believed he was infected by someone, probably his mother, who had touched a dead animal carrying the virus. This is one of the worst outbreaks ever recorded, and it's a new strain. The international health authorities believe the virus is transmitted through bushmeat and that bats are the culprit. From what I've read, following human infection through contact with an infected bat or other wild animal, human-to-human transmission often occurs. Its transmission is a predominant feature of epidemics."

Alfred takes a big, loud sip of his very hot coffee. "She told me last year that while driving between villages on market day, a truck overloaded with fifty men, women, and children and supplies lost control while going down a slight decline. At a curve, the truck smashed into the side of the road, killing most of them instantly; some died later. Rose said she ran out of her truck toward the bodies splattered all over the place, broken and bleeding. A woman, mumbling, stood up and walked toward her, carrying her dead baby. Half of the woman's face was peeled off from her ear to her nose, skin hanging. The mining company in the area immediately deployed medical teams and helicopters to evacuate those who could survive. There were few. You could count them on one hand, she said.

"It was decided that all bodies were to be buried that afternoon. A few bulldozers were sent to the site to begin digging the mass grave. She said bodies were lined up on the ground, which was covered in beautiful African fabrics, and then the final prayer for the dead was delivered. Men circled the bodies, and women circled the men. To release the souls of the dead, Rose said, they united in a somber chant, and she could hear the roar of the bulldozers in the background, waiting for the bodies. One by one, they were placed on a wooden slab and carried to the grave site as the families howled in pain. Then it was over, just like that. Like night and day, she said. Hundreds of people scrambled around as though nothing had happened, running and pushing each other to get into taxis, buses, and the same type of trucks that had just crashed. Hanging bodies and piles of people packed in vehicles, returning to their villages in the same manner that had just killed fifty people from one village. A few months later, Rose went back to the village where this woman lived. She was alive! She was one of the injured who the mining company evacuated."

"Why does she keep going back there?" asks Chester.

"I don't know," replies Alfred, grabbing a doughnut from the table. "Human behavior has always intrigued her. Yet she studies animal behavior, mostly animal-human conflicts."

Eliot walks to the window. The rain has stopped. Alfred finishes eating his doughnut and walks to the window too.

"Eliot, I also came by just to say hi and see if you guys want to join me for lunch before I catch the ferry back to the island. I hate to think what Samuel is up to over there on his own. He met Mrs. Hitchcock; he's making new best friends out there. Everyone just thinks he's a peach." Alfred sounds like a jealous little boy. They all laugh.

"He's a charmer," says Eliot. "Sorry, can't join you. Maybe later. I'd like to finish reading the manuscript. Chester, take him to that little seafood place down the street. It's newly renovated. The father died.

His kids took over and made it a little more modern. You'll like it. The food is wonderful. Keep us informed on how Rose is doing. She's always been a risk taker, that one."

"She calls herself an explorer," says Alfred. "If it gets worse, Jack will pull the plug and get her out of there. If he gets his way, she won't have a choice."

"I doubt he'll be able to drag her out. She's determined. Go away now, and let me finish my work," says Eliot with conviction.

Chester and Alfred take one final look out the window to make sure it's no longer raining. To their surprise, they see Harold walking, feet shuffling, picking away at his nails.

"Hey, Harold!" shouts Chester, waving his arms out the window. Harold looks up, waves back, and keeps walking. "Harold!" repeats Chester, not to be deterred. "Wait for us. Alfred and I are going to Catch for lunch. Wait for us. I'm taking you to lunch."

Verging on falling out the window, Chester slides back in to safety. "Let's go before he runs off."

The door slams shut behind him. Eliot jumps at the abrupt sound. "That fuck! How many times…" He curses under his breath. Shrugging it off, he takes the manuscript and sits comfortably in his favorite chair.

❖ ❖ ❖

CAROLINE: That's quite the performance. I didn't know you were a poet. I hope there's more wherever that came from, my darling! We could also have a songwriter in the making. Better write this stuff down.

TEFERI: He used to write poems all the time. Not sure why you ever stopped.

BEN: I went to med school.

TEFERI: Did you know that some of Ben's poems are in my books? I could use them only as long as I never mentioned who wrote them. But there's no point in keeping that a secret anymore, is there? You just ousted yourself—neurosurgeon-slash-poet. This baby will be either talented or confused. I guess that's what therapy's for.

They all laugh.

CAROLINE: It's time for dessert. Who wants some of Teferi's famous apple pie?

CAROLINE, BEN, TEFERI, JOYCE: Me!

Caroline gets up from the table, takes the dirty plates to the counter, and then takes the pie from the counter and brings it back to the table. As she walks, she notices the calendar marked with an X for each day that's passed and sees scribbling on the whiteboard on the fridge. It's another poem, and it reads:

After such a time
Of fear and sorrow,
Of heartbreak and unknown,
A new relationship grows.

Your friends are near,
Your family close,
Your heart exposed.

Allow this time for life to mend
And see yourself unfold
A new day of hope.

So it is.

SCENE V
CAROLINE AND BEN'S BEDROOM—EVENING

The sound of water filling tub. Ben is resting, Caroline by his side. Facing each other in bed, Caroline talks him through his pain.

CAROLINE: Honey, breathe slowly…You're almost there.

BEN: I can't take this anymore. (*Placing his hands on his head.*) The pain. I'm sorry…

Tears are rolling down his cheeks. Caroline kisses him on the forehead, holding an ice pack on the back of his neck.

CAROLINE: Will you need anything while you're in the tub?

BEN: We are the only authors of our lives. We imagine we know what will be, who we'll be, where we'll be. I remember once when I was on a hike with Teferi and Joyce in the Congo, we came across a low-mountain gorilla. He was lying on his back, stretching his legs and doing all sorts of poses like a yogi. Joyce and I stood there in absolute amazement. He then stood up, faced us, and charged. I'd never seen Joyce move so fast in her life. I'd never followed her so fast in my life either. There we were, both of us up against a tree, hanging on to each other. I thought then that I could never be as scared as I was in that moment. The only thing this gorilla wanted to do was get to his females in the trees behind us. (*Beat.*) I love you so much…Our son…

CAROLINE: He will know you.

Ben makes his way to the bathroom. Caroline remains on the bed, her hand on his pillow. Cut to Ben in the tub, with pen and paper, writing a letter to his son.

SCENE VI
GARDEN—FOUR WEEKS LATER

Joyce is eight months pregnant. Caroline and Joyce are in the garden. Joyce, sitting on her knees, is holding a basket of bulbs. Caroline is planting them.

CAROLINE: I need to go to the market later. We're running out of fruits and vegetables. And then I'll stop by the pharmacy to refill the prescriptions. You feel like coming into town with me later?

JOYCE: No, I'll stay here. Naps are a big thing right now. Teferi hasn't left the house for a while. Take him out with you.

CAROLINE: That's probably a good idea. It's good that he started writing again. When you and Ben were married, why didn't you have any children? I remember you two being so wonderful together, but when I came back from my tour, you were getting divorced.

JOYCE: We were young, Caroline, remember? It was puppy love for us. We married as soon as we were old enough to not need our parents' consent. We talked about having children. We talked about it as a wonderful idea. We talked about it in the same way we talked about buying our first house after he finished med school and we could save up enough money. Ben was really busy with his studies. I went off to shoot a film. Remember? It was my first lead role. That was where I met Tom. He was sitting at the bar in the lodge where we stayed at Kruger National Park. It was love at first sight, and there I was, married to my best friend. I had never experienced anything like it before. The only man I had ever known was Ben. When I came back home, he knew there was something different about me. I couldn't lie to him, and I didn't want to cheat him out of this kind of amazing love because of our sense of obligation to each other. So we let each other go. It was meant to be, because it was at my wedding that you and Ben realized that you two were meant to be together. I have two wonderful children, my best friends are husband and wife, and I am blessed to be able to give you this wonderful gift. I had no idea this could be possible. You know, when you and Ben asked Tom and me, we had no hesitation. By the time these tulips come up, you and Ben will be parents.

CAROLINE: After our fourth miscarriage, the doctor told me there was too much damage, and I could not carry to full term even if I could get pregnant again. He presented us with a couple of options, and somehow Ben knew you would do this for us. When they harvested my eggs to fertilize them with his sperm in the lab and then transplant them into you, I wasn't sure it was going to work. Now here you sit, carrying our child. I have no words, Joyce, that can ever tell you how grateful I am and how happy you have made us. When we found out that it took…that you were pregnant…it was the happiest day of our lives. Then two days later, we get the worst news of our lives. (*Beat.*) So how are those kids of yours enjoying their exchange program in Spain?

JOYCE: Having the time of their lives!

Joyce smiles at Caroline and hands her the last bulb in the basket.

SCENE VII
KITCHEN—LUNCHTIME, SAME DAY

Joyce and Ben are preparing lunch in the kitchen.

BEN: Caroline and I have decided on a name that we think you'll approve of.

JOYCE: Oh yeah? Nothing that will put this poor kid to shame, I hope. I have a few of my own if you need a fallback name when you see his face pop out of me. So tell me, what is it?

BEN: She wanted to wait until the baby was born to tell you, so it could be a surprise, but there's a good chance I won't be there for the momentous event. It's just a few weeks away, and I've already passed my expiration date by a week.

JOYCE: Doctors…they never get the timing right anyway, you know that. Besides, I'm having the baby at home. The midwife is here all the time, getting us ready for this. The baby will be in your hands in no time. Don't tell me the name just yet. Let's wait. Besides, if I don't like the name, I'll just insist on changing it. I'm sure I'll have some kind of say when you see him peeking his little face out of here.

Ben clumsily drops the salad on the ground from laughing. Joyce is too big to bend over to help him pick it up. Ben manages and puts the salad back in the bowl.

JOYCE: It's OK. It's so frickin' clean here, you can drink the toilet water. Caroline has gone crazy with all the organic stuff and keeping the house clinical. They won't know the difference. Add a bit of olive oil and balsamic vinegar, and it's all good.

BEN: I wrote a song for Caroline to record. You want to see it?

JOYCE: Of course.

Ben takes out a folded piece of paper from his back pants pocket. Joyce reads it. Voice of Ben narrating.

Letter to My Son

Your story started a long time ago
I was not your daddy yet
You were more than hope, more than love alone
Your story tells a tale of hope
New life, and new beginnings due to endings

I am your daddy in heaven
I am closer than you know
My hand reaches and touches all your dreams
You will see me in your shadow

I don't know if we'll have the chance to meet
My time is unknown
Each day you grow, my shadow grows

I am your daddy in heaven
I am closer than you know
My hand reaches and touches all your dreams
You will see me in your shadow

Heaven awaits, my son
I am ready
I will find my way
I will find my way back to you
You will know me
In your shadow I will be

In your shadow I will be
In your shadow I will be

Joyce folds the paper and places it on the counter. Joyce and Ben hear the sound of the car pulling up and the doors opening and closing.

SCENE VIII
LIVING ROOM/KITCHEN—LATER, SAME DAY

Teferi and Caroline bring bags of food into the house. Ben is at the door to assist. Joyce is in the living room, preparing cocktails.

JOYCE: (*Shouting from the bar.*) Lunch will be ready in half an hour. Drop those bags and come get your cocktails. I have all of your favorites ready.

Joyce places them all on the bar, each with its own little umbrella. Caroline joins her, still sorting groceries.

JOYCE: Hey…looks like you bought enough food and baby supplies so you never have to leave the house again. Is that your plan? (*Beat.*) Your mother called when you were out. I told her you'd be back late tonight. Have you decided yet if you'll have her come here or go back to Kenya? (*Doesn't wait for a response.*) I've decided to go back to Kenya to meet up with Tom as soon as the doctor says it's OK for me to travel. Also, I'll be using that awesome breast pump you bought a couple weeks ago so this little boy can have a good start, antibodies and all.

CAROLINE: (*Raising her cocktail for a toast.*) To us!

JOYCE: To us!

CAROLINE: I don't know yet what to do about Mother. Did she say what she wanted, or did she just want to chat?

JOYCE: She just wanted to see how things are going. I gave her a full update on the growth and development.

CAROLINE: I heard you get up last night. You haven't been sleeping well this past week.

JOYCE: This boy is active. I think he will keep you up at night. He doesn't move much during the day, but at night it's full-on aerobics. Ben was up as well last night. He hasn't been sleeping as much either.

CAROLINE: I think he's afraid to fall asleep and stay that way. Did you know that the hospital staff has prebooked a hall for a celebration of life instead of a regular funeral service? It was supposed to be this weekend. When he's sleeping, I keep my hand on his chest to make sure his heart is still beating. Teferi also comes into the room a few times throughout the night to check if he's still breathing. Do you know what the plans are for Teferi, once—

JOYCE: I'm not sure. Tom and I invited him to come back to Kenya for a while. The kids will be back; they haven't seen him in a while. He can go on a few safaris with Tom. I'll be going back to work. I received the script today.

CAROLINE: I've been meaning to talk to you about something. Actually, it's more of a favor, and it's a big one. I know you don't want any videos during the delivery, but I was wondering if...oh...I can see in your face already that you're going to say no. Come on, please? It would only be when the baby begins to crown up to when he pops out.

JOYCE: Forget it! No way. The only way that will happen is if you knock me out. No frickin' way.

Laughter.

BEN: What's all the laughing about?

JOYCE: Your wife is trying to get me to agree to being videotaped—or, rather, having my crotch videotaped—for the great crowning!

BEN: Didn't Tom document every moment of your kids' births? I'm sure he showed me the videos. Besides, it's nothing I haven't seen before.

JOYCE: Nice try. No, he did not. Besides, if it's like my other two, it should happen really fast. I'm one of those women who have short labor and fast delivery. And you will all be there to see it.

CAROLINE: Here's your drink, honey. Virgin.

Joyce winks at Ben.

CAROLINE: Weren't you early as well? If I remember, you delivered around eight and a half months.

JOYCE: Yep, that's right, so it could be any day now. Have you noticed that I've dropped? I'm guessing it'll be sooner rather than later. (*Beat.*) Should we have a bet? Date, time, weight? And let's say a hundred bucks for the kitty.

BEN: I say next Thursday, eight o'clock in the morning, seven pounds, four ounces. That's the lucky two-weeks-past-expiration date.

TEFERI: Wow! Seven days—that's quick. (*Beat.*) I bet, knowing Joyce, ten days—Sunday, three o'clock in the morning. And, with the look of that large belly, nine pounds.

JOYCE: Caroline, when do you think you'll be a mommy?

CAROLINE: Hmm…I say Friday night at seven, eight and a half pounds. (*Looking at Joyce.*) And what's your bet?

JOYCE: I'm gonna have to go with Teferi on this one. From the looks of it, this one will be similar to my last two. I'd say Sunday as well. But I don't think he's going to be nine pounds. Goodness, no! This boy feels more like eight pounds, I hope. I'm going to need lots of stretch-mark cream.

Ben's drink drops out of his hand; he falls to one knee.

JOYCE, CAROLINE, TEFERI: Ben!

Teferi and Caroline help Ben to the sofa. Joyce gets Ben's meds from the coffee table. Ben, unconscious for a few seconds, comes to and opens his eyes.

BEN: (*Eyes partially opened.*) I thought I was a goner too, but I have a bet to win first.

Teferi, Caroline, and Joyce giggle nervously.

CAROLINE: Honey, how are you feeling? This is happening more frequently now, about five times a day. (*Beat.*) You guys are not going out tonight. You're staying home.

BEN: Honey, I'm all right.

Ben clumsily tries to sit up. He can't sit up yet.

CAROLINE: I can see that. Have a nap. We'll wake you in an hour. We'll also keep lunch warm for you, and then you can sit with me in the garden. I have more of the small tulips you like so much. Just a few more baskets of bulbs to plant.

BEN: I don't want to sleep. I want to have lunch. Joyce is making me her specialty—a club sandwich and chocolate mousse with strawberries for dessert.

Ben looks down. He's wet himself.

TEFERI: Come on. Let me help you to your room. We'll have a quick wash and change, and then we can have lunch.

SCENE IX
BEN'S ROOM—NOON

Teferi helps Ben undress.

TEFERI: I'll run you a bath. Would you like that?

BEN: Thank you.

Ben sits on the bed while Teferi prepares the bath. Teferi places a stool next to the tub.

TEFERI: I'm putting in some of Caroline's bubble bath.

Ben is sitting naked on the bed, crying quietly. Teferi helps him to the tub.

TEFERI: You want me to put this in the book?

Ben smiles, stands, and then puts his arm around Teferi, who walks him toward the bathroom. Ben stops, puts his other arm around Teferi, and hugs him.

BEN: (*In a low voice.*) Please make sure my son knows who I am.

TEFERI: I will. You have my word.

Teferi helps Ben into the tub.

SCENE X
LIVING ROOM—LATER, SAME DAY

Caroline and Joyce are in the living room. Caroline is looking out the window while Joyce cleans the bar.

JOYCE: Have you decided what you want to do for Ben and Teferi's birthday? Who would have thought? Worlds apart, but born on the very same day. And here they are, waiting for the birth of the baby, which, according to Ben, will happen one day before their birthday.

Joyce walks over to Caroline, who is weeping.

CAROLINE: I think we should have a theme night. All of our favorite foods. What do you think? (*Still weeping.*) Let's have a feast. I want a variety of aromas to fill this house. You can make your delicious triple-layer chocolate cake with the white-chocolate cream sauce, and Teferi can make his famous apple pie. (*Beat.*) Last night in bed, it was like he got a second wind. We made love twice. It's been a while since he's been able to…And just like that he was…well, so horny! I couldn't stop him. It was the hottest sex we've ever had.

JOYCE: Fantastic!

CAROLINE: You're enormous! You sure this baby won't pop out today? (*She sniffles.*) I'm scared, Joyce.

They hug.

JOYCE: Here they come. Let's have lunch.

SCENE XI
LIVING ROOM—DAY BEFORE BIRTHDAY PARTY

Caroline and Teferi are coming into the house with loads of groceries. Ben's appearance makes it obvious that his condition has further deteriorated, but he still manages to get around the house. His adult diaper is sticking out of the back of his pants. A cocktail of drugs lines the side of the kitchen table. Joyce is in the kitchen, cooking up a storm in her enormous, wobbly state.

TEFERI: Hello, we're home! And we have lots of goodies. Ben, come give us a hand.

JOYCE: Hello! I'm in here.

CAROLINE: Wow! It smells wonderful. My mouth is watering. I can't wait for tomorrow. The traffic out there is crazy. I can't believe we've been gone all day.

BEN: Everyone, once all the groceries are brought in, I would like you all to join me in the garden. No questions. Just meet me there in thirty minutes.

Everyone looks at one another, wondering what's going on. Ben makes his way outside.

SCENE XII
BACK GARDEN—EARLY EVENING

Caroline, Teferi, and Joyce make their way to the garden. Before them is a round table covered with food and plenty of wine bottles. Candles light their path, and there are small lights in the trees. A bouquet of tulips adorns the table. Everyone is in awe, surprised by the beauty yet unsure what to make of it.

CAROLINE: What's all this? This is beautiful, honey, but I thought we were having the feast tomorrow night to celebrate both of your birthdays. And how did you manage to get all this done today?

BEN: Shh!

Ben walks over to Caroline, takes her hand, and walks her to the table. He then walks over to Joyce and seats her next to Caroline. Teferi follows and sits next to Joyce. Ben scoops up a wine bottle, already opened, and pours a glass for everyone. He stands for a moment, looking at the others. He's solid—no wobbling or spilling of wine.

BEN: Thank you, Joyce, for helping me today.

Joyce smiles.

BEN: I didn't think I could wait until tomorrow.

Everyone is silent.

CAROLINE: What do you mean? We can always have another party tomorrow. There's plenty of food.

Ben sits next to Caroline and takes her hand.

BEN: I had a dream last night. I was in this garden, sitting with our son. We talked about many things. He also asked if I was ready. Caroline, I won't be here tomorrow. *(Beat.)* Shh, don't cry. Listen to me, my darling. Tonight, we're going to celebrate. I haven't had an appetite like this in a long time.

TEFERI: Hand me your plates. Let's begin.

Ben takes Caroline's plate and hands it to Teferi. Caroline does not take her eyes off Ben. Caroline kisses Ben.

CAROLINE: I love you so much!

Joyce takes her fork and taps her wineglass.

JOYCE: Well…this is going to be quite the send-off. I didn't know this is what you had planned when you asked me to slave away in the kitchen all day.

The four begin the party, with music, eating, and drinking. It goes late into the evening. When the party begins to quiet down, Joyce and Teferi sit quietly on a lounge chair with their feet up. Teferi is massaging her feet. Caroline and Ben are cuddled together on another lounge chair. Then Ben gets up.

BEN: Good night, everyone.

The End

5

It wasn't difficult for Eliot, Jack, and Chester to decide that Felicity was the best and first and *only* choice as lead actress for the film *Write between the Lines*. Like Viviane, the author, Felicity has lived a nightmare and is a heroine. Some believe these women to be vengeful. As a professor at the University of Toronto when she immigrated to Canada after the war, Viviane explored the futility of war in the same vein as Felicity contemplates the vanity of modern medicine and modern medical ethics. Why is it humane to euthanize a cat, a dog, or even an alpaca in an effort to prevent a family pet from suffering? It is in their best interests, they say. It is cruel to let them suffer.

Write between the Lines set out to inform readers of the analogies between God and woman, woman and man, and killing and choosing death. Felicity discovers how one is equipped with the weapons to destroy one's own soul. Whoever killed Viviane's husband also made sure she was equally discredited. But their attempt was to no avail. Viviane's ability to influence was evident through her wit and gentle touch, further provoking her husband's murderers.

From two different worlds, each woman made a telling point, using a central theme, while never seeking redemption for their choice, their act to end a life. While on trial for murder, both women strenuously opposed a guilty plea of murder and squashed the gratifying vanity of their accusers. The vision—the memory of vomit, of torture, of screams—was never going to be an imitation of anything else but rather a duty of the cancer that ate away at Luc's body. Felicity and Luc had no self-deception of the reality that faced them. As did Viviane—only a deep awareness of consciousness, of self, existed, and choices needed to be made without doubt or regret.

"Luc, dinner is ready." Felicity put the beautiful plate of sliced roast beef surrounded with carrots and potatoes on the table. Poured wine into two glasses. "Luc, dinner," she called out again. Wheeling behind him an IV bag, Luc quietly entered the kitchen and sat at the dinner table.

"Wow, this looks delicious, Mom." Felicity smiled and sat across from him.

"And I've made your favorite dessert." She pointed to the pie on the counter. "Maple syrup pie. I made it this morning when you were at the clinic."

"Mom. We need to talk," Luc said as he attempted to cut his meat without the IV tube getting in the way.

"Honey, can we eat now and talk after dinner? I've poured you a tiny bit of red wine. Just enough to wet your lips." She raised her glass to make a toast. "Honey, raise your glass."

"Mom, OK, but we talk right after this toast." He slowly reached for his crystal goblet on the table next to his plate, close to the edge of the table. Felicity had placed everything close enough to make it an easy reach for him.

"OK. To us. To you, my darling boy." She raised her glass proudly.

"Mom, I'm seventeen and a half. You don't need to keep calling me your darling boy." He smirked. "To us." Luc slowly sipped his wine, savoring the drop sitting on the edge of his lips. "Mom." Too weak to keep holding the glass, Luc placed the goblet back on the table.

"Yes." Felicity cut into her roast and brought the fork to her mouth.

"Remember when I first got sick, and I told you I would go as far as I can with this?"

"Honey, this is not right. We shouldn't be thinking about this. We don't know what medical discoveries can be made at any time." She put her fork down next to her plate.

"I know, but we've talked about this several times, and I'm always sure of my decision. And I wasn't just talking about it because I had nothing else to talk about. I know you didn't take me seriously all those times, but I want you to take me seriously now. After my treatment at the clinic this morning, I went to see a lawyer."

Felicity was frustrated. "Why would you do that, and how did you find a lawyer, and what did you talk about?"

"Mom, I know this is very upsetting for you, but I really need your support. I really need your help because I can't do it myself."

"We still have some time before we even have to think about this. Eat your dinner." Felicity pointed firmly at his plate.

"Jack."

"What do you mean, Jack?" asked Felicity.

"It's Jack who referred me to a lawyer." Sitting there with a smug look on his face, he said, "I told you he was going to do this."

"He has no business doing this. I'll talk to Jack myself." She cut briskly into her very tender roast.

"Mom. The lawyer will help me. We've already drafted a letter. It's part of my will and testament. It's all official…you know what I mean?"

"I'm not happy with this, and I'm not doing this. I'm sorry. But my answer is no!"

"OK, well…there's something else I want to talk to you about." Luc fiddled around with his IV tube as he cut and ate his food.

"What's that?" She was still frustrated.

"How come you never told me that Jack was my father, well…the sperm donor?" Luc sat back in his chair, taking a rest from eating.

"What do you mean?"

"It's a simple question, Mom. Why didn't you ever tell me he was my father?"

"Is that what he said to you?" Felicity took a big gulp of her wine.

"No, but it's obvious. We look exactly alike, we have the same mannerisms, and we even have the same voice. Also, I saw a baby picture of him with his mom—or should I say Grandma. It was on his desk. I'm not sure if he takes more pride in that photo or the one of Oscar

Wilde mounted on his wall. Mom, my baby photos look exactly like him at that age."

"Luc, that was a long time ago. We had been working together for over fifteen years by then, and I wanted a child. I wanted you. I was single—"

"Mom, I know the story. You told me like a hundred times. I'm not upset. It's just that Jack has been in my life since I was born. Why—"

"Luc, it's an arrangement, an agreement that I asked of Jack. He's always been there for us." Felicity sat back in her chair, sipping her wine.

"Mom, it's OK. I'm just glad that it's him." Luc smiled at Felicity to reassure her.

"Does Jack know you know?"

"No, no yet." Luc reached slowly for his wine. "Mom, I think this is enough for me tonight. Can you help me with one last tiny sip? I'd like to lie down right now."

"Of course, my darling." Felicity helped him with his wine and helped him to the sofa in the living room. "I'll bring you your piece of pie in a few minutes." Felicity arranged the pillow under his head and back.

"Thanks, Mom."

❖ ❖ ❖

Felicity does not see herself as Viviane but as someone who has become a central character in Felicity's life, which is necessary for the leading actress. Felicity is honest enough, wise enough, and passive enough to question and understand the narrative of this woman's life, which she is about to make come to life once again. As a girl, Felicity observed how adults shrewdly sensed they were entitled to the carnage they left behind. And those sitting on the fence lived in a world of exaltation and terror, confusing their sins with good deeds.

In each of the women's modern worlds, the authorities unraveled their lives. Felicity's and Viviane's reputations were deemed obscene; they defied man's mortal version of freedom of choice and God's meaning of free will. Naturally citizens believed themselves qualified to provide the necessary critiques to establish censorship in an attempt to cast the first stone, leaving Felicity and Viviane exposed with acute precision. Religion is flawed; God is outstandingly perfect.

Both women put their faith only in God, who reminded them of whom they were meant to be. They could cope with the images of their own conditions, their choices, and believed no other. They were to be graded and measured, their creator highlighting their injustices. That they could accept.

❖ ❖ ❖

There is a calmness after the storm. The sea is still. Alfred walks up on deck. His beautiful, chocolate-brown eyes twitch from the glare of the brilliant water below. He wonders how he gets on in this world. Is it better to let one go insane, embrace lunacy, or accept life as it is, as a sane man? What does God want from Harold? What does God want of him?

Felicity remains certain of her destiny. Samuel is oblivious to his or to anything at all, so it seems. God he never mentions. Alfred remembers the summer they spent together at the lake when they were boys. Samuel refused to go to church on Sundays.

"I will not betray my best friend." Samuel pointed up at the heavens.

They pass the islands and are out at sea. Felicity's self-confinement to the island and her theatre allows her to recover. Alfred observes that a woman refusing to ride sidesaddle is still judged by society as not obedient. A woman's survival weighs heavily on whether or not she is considered a lady or horsey, gulping whiskey instead of sipping wine.

Of course, without a doubt, the fall of Adam was due to Eve's transgressions of theological principles. The lopsided view of scripture, which was written and interpreted by man, is, many think, without a doubt that women brought sin into the world and therefore are in a perpetual state of punishment for sin. Thus it is unfitting for these sinful mortals to be chosen as channels of God's grace.

As a result, God reprimands woman by multiplying her pain in childbirth, never considering Adam as the one deceiving him. Rational thought is completely dismissed by man without repentance. Emilia's monologue in *Othello* eloquently expresses her view of such dismissal:

> Yes, a dozen; and as many to the vantage as would
> Store the world they played for.
> But I do think it is their husbands' faults
> If wives do fall: say that they slack their duties,
> And pour our treasures into foreign laps,
> Or else break out in peevish jealousies,
> Throwing restraint upon us; or say they strike us,
> Or scant our former having in despite;
> Why, we have galls, and though we have some grace,
> Yet have we some revenge. Let husbands know
> Their wives have sense like them: they see and smell
> And have their palates both for sweet and sour,
> As husbands have. What is it that they do
> When they change us for others? Is it sport?
> I think it is: and doth affection breed it?
> I think it doth: isn't frailty that thus errs?
> It is so too: and have not we affections,
> Desires for sport, and frailty, as men have?
> Then let them use us well: else let them know,
> The ills we do, their ills instruct us so.

Meow…meow…meow.

Alfred looks down into his jacket pocket at the tiny kitten he rescued from a drainage pipe near where he parked his car while in town. He brings the silver-and-black-striped tabby to his chin, stroking her, keeping her close, away from the cool sea breeze. From his side pocket, Alfred removes a tiny container of milk he had taken from the ferry cafeteria, strips back the plastic cover, and presents the tiny milk cup to the kitten. With no hesitation the kitten laps it all up, leaving milk droplets all over his face, looking content.

"You're going to be a great mouser, little one. Felicity will love you."

Meow. The kitten wiggles in closer, under Alfred's jacket, and goes to sleep.

Gulls appear overhead, very close, shitting on people.

"Must be getting close to the island," Alfred observes. The birds hone in on the fries dangling from fingers, thieves in flight, signaling an end to Alfred's sea journey.

The sudden jolt of the anchor rolling out of the vessel, grabbing the earth, rocks the passengers. Unsteady are their feet. Everyone is ready to exit the ferry. Columns of cars, engines rumbling, all waiting for instructions to disembark. The structure by which Alfred contemplates the modern world teaches him to strip away slaved beliefs and ideals. In comparison Samuel prefers to project his moral values and cultural beliefs, to animate his spirit, by watching the response. Occasionally believing himself to be a prophet in his own right, Samuel discernibly embodies only the abstract responses. This annoys Alfred to no end. Able to foretell Samuel's next move, he exhausts all possibilities by strategically positioning himself beautifully, without enslaving himself to Samuel's next move. Checkmate!

Enchanted by Felicity's beauty, she evokes her symmetry, leaving Samuel observant, intrigued, and provoked.

Go away, go away…

*Honk…honk…honk…*Alfred snaps out of his meditation, visualizing Samuel gone when he gets home. He is next up to drive off the ship, and the crew is frantically waving. He takes the car out of park, steps on the gas pedal, and slowly moves forward off the ship.

Alfred meanders up the newly paved road, longing for Felicity; he has an evening planned with wine and seafood, alone by the fire. Alfred feels the vibration of the purring in his coat pocket. Scratching to escape and have a peek at her new world, the kitten pokes her head out with great curiosity.

"Matilda. That's your name. Matilda." Alfred pats her on the head. "Just a little longer."

He pulls into the parking lot of the seafood market to buy dinner for the evening. "Stay right here. I'll be just a minute," he assures Matilda as he places her on the passenger seat, wrapping her in a blanket from the backseat. "I'll get you a treat," he promises.

Alfred, like a worried new father, glances back to the car's passenger-side window to look in on Matilda one last time before entering the store.

"Long time no see, Alfred," says Carl, the store's owner, from behind the counter. "What can I do for you today?"

"Good day, Carl. How are you?" Alfred responds, scanning the fish, which are perfectly stretched out on ice.

"Samuel was here this morning," Carl says. "He bought enough fish to feed the entire village."

Alfred stops scanning, pausing in position, and takes a deep breath. "You don't say."

"Yes," says Carl. "Apparently, he's organizing a town picnic."

Alfred snuffles, placing his hands in his pockets, trying to relax his fists.

"You must be happy to have him around. He's been making the rounds in town, making friends with everyone. He's quite the character."

"Yeah, I'm just so lucky," Alfred says sarcastically under his breath. "He's been with us for over a month. Is there anything he didn't get that I can bring home for tonight's dinner?" He takes a sample of the Indian candy on the counter. Dried, smoked salmon with maple syrup—his favorite. He wraps a few more pieces in a napkin for Matilda.

Since their childhood, Samuel had always gotten what he wanted and done what he wanted, according to Alfred. He wanted to be teacher's pet, and he was; he wanted to be school president, and he was; he wanted the girl, and he got her, no matter if Alfred saw her first. Alfred believed that Samuel just went along and thought only of himself without ever worrying about what anyone else wanted or thought, which infuriated Alfred. But there was a bond between the two boys, one that even Alfred could not deny. When Alfred first arrived at the boarding school, Samuel had already been there a few months. Samuel had recently moved to England from Canada, from an island on the west coast of British Columbia. They were both seven years old; Samuel was a few months older than Alfred. Alfred was a shy and nervous boy who didn't really know how to make friends. He was and still is an introvert with little desire to have people around him most times. Alfred preferred to spend most of his time alone, reading or being with nature, exploring what insects and other wild creatures were doing. However, Alfred's path was written: he was to take over the family business, the corporation established in the early 1800s by his great-grandparents.

Samuel, on the other hand, was an intellect, a voracious reader, but an extrovert and curious about everything and everyone; he couldn't get enough of people. He sees and reads people within seconds of meeting them. He felt obliged to reach out to Alfred, out of consideration for him, to ensure that he would not be alone and would know right away that he had a friend. And he's been there for Alfred ever since, through every trial and tribulation, every cut and scratch, every breakup, every death; and Alfred had mourned more than his share for a boy his age. After a few months of hanging out together every day, Samuel managed to get Alfred to talk about himself, and this is when he learned that Alfred had a twin sister, Joy, who had died in a plane crash when she was six years old. The loss did not end with Alfred's twin sister; his grandparents had been with Joy, and they had also died in the crash.

As the years passed, the two boys were inseparable until Alfred moved to Canada. The guys would get together for every birthday, holiday, and any other reason they could find just to go on crazy holidays in remote parts of the world—until Alfred's father passed away. Duty called for Alfred, and he was forced to leave his crazy, wild adventures behind. Samuel still always made a point to visit Alfred at every birthday and holiday, but they were more quiet and subdued get-togethers. When Alfred met Felicity, he waited a year before introducing her to Samuel. Still insecure with women, especially when it came to Samuel, Alfred feared losing his leading lady to him just by sheer animal attraction. Samuel did not need to say a word or do anything; women were drawn to him like moths to a flame, which always resulted in tragedy for the girl because Samuel would never commit. He always remained faithful when he was with someone, but never gave her his heart. It was as though he were saving it for someone.

Alfred could not put his finger on it; he couldn't figure out what was going on with Samuel despite probing him with millions of questions. Samuel had given Alfred plenty of reasons in the past to have suspicions even if Felicity never gave Samuel a second thought. Samuel had left Alfred with enough cause for concern, and he didn't want history repeating itself. He hated leaving Samuel alone with Felicity in fear that somehow he would work his voodoo on her and she would be taken in by his spell. Alfred was anxious to get home to break up whatever his paranoid mind was imagining could be happening at the beach house.

"Just that," Carl says, pointing to the Indian candy. "He didn't get any of that candy. It wasn't in yet. He purchased many different herbs, mixes, and sauces, though."

Alfred eats a few more pieces of candy, leaving only a couple for other customers, to show that he has not eaten the entire portion. Then he changes his mind. There is no one else in the store, it is near closing, and he figures no one else will be coming in, so he snatches them from the plate and places them gently in his mouth, savoring every morsel.

"Give me what's left. I'll have some for a few days." Alfred points to the remaining Indian candy under the glass counter. Carl hands him the large and small pieces, finely wrapped.

"Fifty dollars, please," says Carl.

Alfred removes a fifty-dollar bill from his wallet and hands it to Carl. "Hey, would you like to see the queen's bum?"

"What? Of course I'd like to see the queen's bum," Carl says with a chuckle. "Where's the viewing?"

"Right here." Alfred removes a five-dollar note from his wallet, folds the portion of the queen's face below her chin, creating a slight double chin. "There it is!" he proclaims innocently and giggles as he chews on his candy.

"Wonderful!" Carl laughs. "It's so childish that it's hilarious. I love it. I'll have to show my kids when I get home tonight. They'll love it."

"Thanks again," Alfred says, raising his bag of candy as he walks out the door.

"Drive carefully; the fog is rolling in," says Carl.

"Will do, thanks," Alfred replies, concerned, as he looks out at the sea. The fog is rolling in quite fast. For years Alfred has seen the fog dissipate as fast as it's rolled in. As a precaution, he decides to wait out the fog at the local pub just around the bend from the seafood store, despite his eagerness to get home and break up whatever passionate lovemaking could be going on in his absence. Before leaving the car, he checks in on little Matilda and leaves her with a few savory morsels of Indian candy.

The quiet bar is beautifully adorned with dark wood carvings along the beams. The most comfortable seat in the corner by the window lures him in.

"What can I serve you?" calls out the bartender.

"Cranberry juice, please."

The bartender pours the cranberry cocktail into his finest pint glass and carries it out to Alfred.

"Here you go, Alfred. You've come in just in time. The fog is rolling in and fast."

"I see. I was on my way home. Business on the mainland for a few days." He takes a sip of his cranberry juice. "Thank you. Just what I need."

Alfred drinks eagerly from his tall pint glass, looking out the window with a sigh. Samuel plagues his mind.

Why? he wonders. *What sin have I committed to deserve such punishment?*

A mild fire crackles, warming the room just right. Alfred rests his head back. Too bad Carl doesn't have any of that poisonous fish. *If not cooked right…*he fantasizes with a smirk. The bartender tapping a newspaper on his forehead snaps him out of his daydream.

"Have you seen this?" The bartender places the newspaper, folded to the front page, on the table next to the cranberry juice. The headline reads, "The World's Deadliest Outbreak of the Ebola Virus." Sierra Leone is now the epicenter of the ebola outbreak. Liberia closed its borders. American doctors are contaminated, dying of disease…

"Any news on Rose?" asks the bartender. "Jack will no doubt be worried."

Rose. Where is Rose? Alfred wonders, concerned. He immediately sends a text message to Jack.

"Jungle, Congo, tracking gorillas," replies Jack in a text.

"Keep us posted," Alfred texts back.

He looks up at the bartender and raises his iPhone. "She's in the Congo tracking gorillas."

"Well, at least she's out of there for now." The bartender refills Alfred's glass with cranberry juice.

Sipping his juice Alfred deliberates on human history, its repetitive points and purposes, enduring tolerance of suffering, especially inflicting suffering. Smaller print at the bottom of the front page reads, "Tragedy continues in Guinea. Thirty-six children killed in stampede at concert." A people, a nation, forced to endure defeat, loss, never victorious over a corrupt government, the military, the police, individuals, tribal conflicts, and their own family members. Can those with contemplative minds help free the people who pervade, secretly wanting democracy, justice, a right to a good life?

The fog rolls in, calling back a memory. Alfred was looking for her, calling out her name. Walking through the forest, the sea pounding against the rocks, ferns covering her body, Samuel was next to her. Alfred loved her; he didn't. Would he take Felicity away from him as well? Alfred would never know. His first love, dead at the age of twelve.

Time to get back to Matilda and head home to be with his lovely Felicity and the unavoidable Samuel. But the thick fog covers the pub windows. Visibility is zero. Delay is inevitable.

"Looks like you're here for a little while," says the bartender. "Want something else instead?"

Alfred tells him about Matilda, alone in the car.

"Bring her in," the bartender replies. "I'll prepare a saucer of milk for her."

Alfred opens the pub door. He can't see a thing. One step into the fog, he presses the car key's unlock button—*click*—making the car's headlights flash on and off, acting as a beacon. He slowly heads in the direction of the lights and walks right into the car. Feeling his way around it, he opens the door and searches for Matilda, wrapped in the blanket on the passenger seat. She is fast asleep; he wakes her and puts her in his coat pocket. After closing the car door, he turns toward the pub. Alfred takes a few steps forward, but he's unsure if he's heading in the right direction. He searches in the distance for the small light above the bar's door. He feels a bit disoriented. He stands still. It's cold. Matilda, tucked away in his warm coat pocket, is asleep, unaware of the situation.

"Alfred," a melodious, siren-like voice calls from a distance. Alfred, startled, looks around in the fog, confused.

"Who's there?" he calls out and takes a few more small steps toward what he hopes is the pub. He knows of the legend of the mermaids coming to shore only when the fog rolls in, to avoid being seen.

Is this one of them? he wonders. Then, realizing he must be imagining it, he continues in the same direction toward the bar. Suddenly, in the distance, Alfred sees what looks like a woman standing on the edge of the cliff.

"Who's there?" he calls out. The woman doesn't move or respond. Alfred, terrified, realizes he's been heading in the wrong direction.

"Alfred! Alfred! Alfred!" the bartender calls out.

Alfred quickly turns around and shouts, "I'm here."

"Follow my voice. Over here, over here."

Alfred begins to see the light above the pub door and lets out a sigh of relief. He looks back to where the woman was standing. The fog is too thick; he cannot see her. Not knowing whether she can hear him, he calls out in a grateful tone, "Thank you."

"You're welcome," shouts the bartender. "Keep coming this way. I can hear you. You're getting closer…There you are." The bartender reaches out to him. "What happened out there? I figured you might have taken a wrong turn. I need to change this light. It needs to be brighter." He points to the light above the door. "Come in and show us this little beauty. Matilda, you say? Is that her name?"

Alfred, safely back in the pub, removes Matilda from his coat pocket.

"Hello, little one. Here's some nice warm milk for you. Put her here," the bartender says, pointing next to the fireplace. "Looks like you're here for a while. Would you like something a little stronger than that cranberry juice? Something to warm your blood?"

Alfred sits back in his chair, speechless, in shock at what has just occurred.

"So, what would you like, Alfred?" asks the bartender. "You look a bit…hmmm, strange. Something happen out there?"

"Hot chocolate, please," replies Alfred.

"Would you like a bit of something else with that cocoa, for a bit of a kick?"

"No, thank you." Alfred, still in a daze, stares at Matilda drinking her milk.

"I know what it is," says the bartender. "You saw one of those sirens, didn't you? My grandfather told me all about them. I'm waiting for one of them to walk into the bar. Now, that would be something, wouldn't it?"

The bartender places a cup of hot cocoa on the table in front of Alfred.

"But as long as I know they're out there and they've got my back, I'm good with that as well. When Samuel came by the other day, he asked me about them. You have an interesting friend, Alfred. You're lucky to have him. He just thinks the world of you."

"Oh yeah?" says Alfred and sips his hot cocoa. "What do you mean they've got your back?"

"Well, you know. Have you seen that cliff out there?" Not waiting for an answer, the bartender continues, "Doesn't matter what's done to prevent people from going as close as possible. They still tempt fate and walk right to the edge to see what's below, despite all the barriers and warning signs. Grandfather says the mermaids watch out for those idiots. Not sure why, but they do. We've had, over the years, a few people who have fallen in, and somehow they were brought back to shore safely, though frightened and coughing up half the sea they've swallowed. There's no way anyone once down there can swim back on his own.

They're usually hanging for dear life on the edges of the rocks until a coast guard helicopter comes to their rescue." The bartender remembers the food cooking in the kitchen. "There's stew heating up on the stove. Would you like a bowl? I don't think you'll make it home for dinner."

"Yes, please, thank you," replies Alfred.

"You're also welcome to use the spare room up on the first floor in case this fog doesn't lift until morning."

"I don't think that will be necessary, but thank you for the kind offer," replies Alfred.

Leaving Samuel alone with Felicity for another night is not what Alfred has in mind for the evening. But he's concerned that the fog is so thick and doubts that it's going to dissipate anytime soon. He hates to admit to himself that it will be a while before anyone can get back on the road. He is only thirty minutes away from home, and tonight it feels like an eternity. Leaning back in his chair next to the window, he looks out to see if the mermaid is there. White, thick fog reveals nothing. Alfred drifts off.

❖ ❖ ❖

"Wake up. Here's a nice, warm cup of coffee," offers the bartender as he taps Alfred on the shoulder. "You slept like the dead. I couldn't wake you."

Alfred opens his eyes. A warm wool blanket is draped over him, and Matilda is on his lap.

"I'm sorry. Please forgive me," he says, straightening himself up in the chair. He takes Matilda into his hands and removes the blanket. "What time is it?"

"Six o'clock in the morning," replies the bartender. "Here's your coffee. Give her to me. I have breakfast ready for Matilda." He takes the kitten from Alfred.

"Felicity! She must be sick with worry," says Alfred anxiously.

"I called her last night when I couldn't wake you," says the bartender. "She's expecting you this morning."

"Thank you." Alfred sips his coffee and looks out the window.

"Lovely morning." The bartender places a plate of toast and jam on the table. "Eat up."

"Thank you," says Alfred.

He eats his toast and drinks his coffee quietly. "Time to go, Matilda." He takes her into his arms. "Thank you for your hospitality," he tells the bartender. "What do I owe you?"

"Nothing. Thank you for coming by. Now you can make it home safely. See you again soon."

The bartender walks Alfred to the door. "Drive safely." He smiles at Alfred, who expresses his gratitude once again and heads out.

On his way to the car, he decides to continue toward the cliff—not too close, but close enough to thank her once again. "Thanks for not letting me tumble to my death and Matilda's," Alfred whispers so no one hears him talking into the air. He looks out onto the sea, standing close enough to the edge of the cliff for the mermaid to hear him, he hopes, but far enough so he's not one of those idiots found washed up on the cliff face, hanging on for dear life.

❖ ❖ ❖

Back on the road, Alfred tells Matilda the story of the mermaid. Matilda sits quietly, listening to every word, with a few meows mixed in the conversation.

Buzz…buzz…

Alfred looks down at his phone on the seat next to Matilda. A call from Jack. He pulls over to the side of the road and answers his phone.

"Hi, Jack, how's everything? Any more news from Rose?"

"Good morning. Yes! She's coming home."

"Wonderful. We'll all be glad to see her. And I'm sure she'll have a great piece of work to prepare. She's an excellent documentary filmmaker, that sister of yours."

"Yes, she is, but she worries us too much in the process," says Jack, sounding both frustrated and relieved.

"Felicity will be glad to see her again. When can we expect her?" asks Alfred.

"One week from today."

"Lovely. We look forward to seeing you both at the house."

"You think Felicity is ready to see me?" Jack asks in a concerned voice.

"The timing is right, Jack. I wouldn't worry about it. You know how much she loves Rose. She loves you as well. She just needed this time to herself."

"Of course. I understand. Is Samuel still with you at the beach house?"

"Yes. I think he'll be with us for a while. Apparently, he's planning a community barbecue."

"He's always doing something like that, isn't he?"

"Yep. Well, that's great news, Jack. I'm happy to hear our little Rose will soon be back home. Felicity is waiting, so I must get back on the road. Give me a call in a few days, and I'll certainly see you next weekend. Plan on staying the entire weekend. We'd love to have you both," says Alfred, anxious to get home to Felicity.

"Thank you. See you next weekend. Good-bye, Alfred."

❖ ❖ ❖

The twist and turns of the road, hugging the coastline, alone with the sea, put Alfred in a hypnotic state on his return home to his huldra. Priceless pages of love poems, love letters, and love songs. Spiritual essence of eternal wisdom. Speculation. Nervous apology for a chaotic experience. Jealousy. Instead, imitators of control, of significance, a contemporary life. Nightmare. By way of compensation, realism, a version of the real world, artificially transformed into something believable. The contrast of a photograph taken of his life, so a sophisticated audience can share in understanding his existence. Alfred's view of love, as an affirmation of the soul's annotated soliloquy, searching for a beginning, what would it be, what utterance expressed?

He muses over the impression of himself, his reflection as a legitimate reincarnation from the carnage of many years of believing he is complex. Sudden sabotage, unable to douse the unconscious mind, judging it ill bred. How, and by which gestures possible, can he release his own tyrannical hold of unyielding certainty? Samuel, consistently showing pleasure by displaying the nuts and bolts of the most intricate contraption: the heart. Never concealing, working all the tricks, and sharing all the philosophies with any audience interested in knowing how and why he places himself as a central character with no commas, disbelieving everything that removes romance, so it can take on a life of its own. Congruent with the politics of criticism, modern self-expression of romanticism gives a sense of ending, with a clear distinction between myth and fiction. Fantasy. Samuel's attempts at defeating everyday myths over plots, compensating the unpredictability against resistance from his own truth.

Suddenly, as he meanders around the next turn, his attention is drawn by waving arms. A man is standing near a car with the hood raised. Signaling, Alfred pulls over. But before he comes to a full stop, the man runs toward him.

"I'm so happy to see someone," the man says as he leans against the car window.

"Francis, what are you doing out here?" asks Alfred.

"Alfred, hi, good to see you. I was on my way to your beach house," Francis replies. "I ran out of gas, can you believe it!"

"How is it that you can leave the house in that very expensive Ferrari and run out of gas? I've never heard of that before. There's a jerrican in the back. Get it, and I'll siphon enough fuel to get you to the next station. Why are you on the way to my house anyway? Especially so early in the morning?"

"It's a beautiful morning. I felt like going for a drive, and I thought I would drop in to say hi. It's been a while since I've seen Samuel. Felicity mentioned that he's staying with you. I don't get to see much of her either, so I thought I'd come by to visit with all of you."

"She'll be happy to see you again. Apparently, Samuel is cooking up a storm tonight. Are you spending the night?" asks Alfred.

"If you don't mind."

"Not at all." Alfred removes the jerrican nozzle from Francis's Ferrari. "You're ready to go. The gas station is just a few kilometers up ahead, on your right. I'll be right behind you."

"Thank you. See you there." Francis gets into his car and drives away.

Alfred follows, irked that once again his restful plans with Felicity on their sailboat have been botched. His internal rage draws him back in to his hypnotic state, his world view, the ever-repeating monologue of his greatest uncontrollable fear of losing Felicity and jealousy of Samuel. Unexpectedly, a small rock smacks the car windshield, shocking him into a sudden stop. Without warning a large rock mass rolls down the cliff, onto the road. Alfred sees a massive rock clip the back end of Francis's car, causing it to spin out of control and slam into the cliff wall. Alfred, struggling to retain control of his vehicle, surprisingly manages to drive out of the danger zone. Within seconds it's over. He pulls off onto the side of the road. Fearful for Francis's safety, he carefully gets out of the car and runs to his aid. He sees an arm struggling to free itself from the car window.

"Get me out of here," moans Francis.

Alfred manages to yank open the car door and pulls Francis out of the semicrushed car. He helps Francis walk to his Land Rover.

"Are you hurt anywhere, Francis?" asks Alfred, concerned, examining every inch of Francis.

"No, just shaken up." Francis is barely able to stand on his own, looking dazed and confused at the wreckage.

"Look, I need to get you in the car so we can get out of here. We don't know when the next slide will come," Alfred says with urgency.

He gets Francis into the car and lays him down in the backseat. "Rest here a minute. I'll call 9-1-1 to report the rockslide. I also need to make sure that no one else is coming from either direction. I have emergency warning triangles in the back. I need to put them out on the road quickly. I'll be right back."

❖ ❖ ❖

Felicity looks up at the clock in the kitchen. It's been over an hour since Alfred called to say that he'd left the pub. *It shouldn't take more than thirty minutes*, she recalls. Anxious, she tidies up the house. Samuel is out in the yard. His shirt hangs off the kitchen chair. Felicity takes the shirt, examines it. *Same taste in style as Luc*, she thinks, reflecting on the times she used to help dress him.

"Time to get up, Luc," she called out from behind the closed bedroom door. *Knock, knock, knock.* "Can I come in? Luc, time to get up. Your appointment is an hour." No reply from inside the bedroom. Felicity slowly opened the door. "Honey, can I come in?" No reply. "Luc, I'm coming in."

She poked her head into the bedroom and found Luc unconscious, partially on the bed, partially fallen forward onto the floor. The bed and his pajamas were soiled with urine and feces. Felicity ran to Luc, lifting him off the floor and putting him back onto the bed. She took the phone from the end table to call 9-1-1.

❖ ❖ ❖

Beep…beep…beep…

Luc slowly opened his eyes. "Honey, I'm here. You're at the hospital." Felicity sat on the edge of the bed, stroking his black hair. She remembered how strong he was. His athletic body growing into a man. His passion for piano, playing for hours upon hours since the age of five instead of playing sports. Luc looked up at her, his eyes watering, and a tear rolled down his cheek.

"Honey, you're OK. You had one of your episodes. The doctor warned us that this would happen. The doctor said you can come home tomorrow." She smiled at him and kissed his forehead. Luc, exhausted, looked up from the tubes branching out of his body to the machines next to his bed. He looked back at his mother, his eyes begging her to put an end to all this senseless suffering.

❖ ❖ ❖

Alfred, apprehensive and frightened, grabs the triangles from the back of the car. He looks up at the cliff—no falling rocks. The ten-meter stretch around the bend seems like an eternity. He runs as fast as he can around the fallen rocks and debris to reach the other side. No oncoming vehicles. He quickly places the triangles in the middle of the road, far enough away from the rocks, before anyone can reach the danger zone around the corner. In a panicked state, needing to tempt fate once again, he runs as fast as he can back to the car while looking up at the cliff. Safely back at the car, he jumps in and slams down on the accelerator.

Bewildered by the events of the last twenty-four hours, Alfred anxiously rubs his forehead, pondering his life expectancy. Is his expiration date approaching? He can't help thinking that things come in threes. He has only a short distance to go before he will be home.

As he approaches the nearby gas station, an ambulance follows suit from the opposite direction. Alfred flashes his headlights like a disco ball, waving his arm frantically out the car window, signaling the ambulance driver to stop. The driver pulls up next to Alfred's car. By the time Alfred steps out, the paramedics are already approaching him.

"He's in the backseat," Alfred says, taking short, rapid breaths. He opens the back door. Francis lies there conscious, with Matilda on his chest.

"Alfred, where did you get this beauty?" asks Francis.

"What? The ambulance is here, Francis. They need to examine you," Alfred replies in a bit of a daze.

He takes Matilda from Francis. "I'm sorry, Matilda. I'm glad to see you're OK." Alfred cuddles her and then places her in his coat pocket.

The paramedics help Francis out of the car to the ambulance. After a full exam, he insists on being released, convincing the paramedics there is no need for him to go to the hospital.

"Francis, are you sure you don't want to go?" says Alfred.

"It's just a few cuts and bruises. I'm OK." Francis points to the butterfly bandage on his forehead. "We need to call Felicity."

"I already did. I've explained everything. I told her to stay home. Samuel will make sure she stays put."

"Alfred. Oh my God, Alfred, are you OK?" a voice cries out.

He turns to see who's calling out to him. "Mrs. Hitchcock. Yes, we're fine."

"I was on my way to the gas station when I heard on the radio that there was a rockslide at Salmon Bend. If it weren't for the emergency triangles you left on the road, others would not have been so lucky. The top of the cliff crumbled, releasing massive boulders and trees, splitting the road in two when they hit the ground."

Alfred and Francis remain silent, feeling very fortunate.

"Mrs. Hitchcock," Alfred says, "this is Francis, Felicity's cousin."

Francis puts out his hand. "Nice to meet you."

"Likewise," she says.

"Mrs. Hitchcock, please drive carefully. I need to get him home. Felicity is waiting for us." Alfred excuses himself and helps Francis from the ambulance.

"Of course. Please let me know if you need anything. Drive carefully as well."

Before leaving, Mrs. Hitchcock assists Alfred with Francis.

"Thank you, Mrs. Hitchcock, but please, no need to trouble yourself. As you can see, Francis is a tall, solid man. He's just a bit shaken up. I would feel more at ease if I could make sure you got home safely as well."

Mrs. Hitchcock concedes to his wishes and returns to her car. She gets a bag labeled "Hitchcock Buns" and a small parcel, backs out of the car, and returns to Alfred.

"Please, take this. This is for Felicity." She hands him the bag and shows him the parcel with Felicity's name on it.

"Thank you, Mrs. Hitchcock. Please, drive safely, and we'll see you soon. Come by the house anytime."

Alfred waits until she drives away before leaving the gas station.

"Here, take this." He hands the baked goods to Francis. "Best pastries you'll ever have."

Alfred drives off, hoping nothing else will happen to prevent him from arriving home. "Call Felicity. Tell her we'll be home in fifteen minutes."

6

The language in which the universe chooses to express to Alfred the notions of life and death eludes him. He would prefer an echo of the boorishness of jealousy displayed, the weariness of ownership imposed, suspicion suffocating his vision, never allowing the present to be. Essential embrace, making it possible to write his own life story, a better one than what he would have told. Why had he not taken that step over the cliff? Why had the cliff not fallen on his head? How is it that the precipice of life allows him to balance on its edge, never letting him perish? The making of life, rivaling the unexpected, the unknown, its mortal finality. Alfred now understands that Luc did not choose death. He chose life.

Finally, home sweet home, thinks Alfred. Up on the left, he spots the driveway leading him to his Shangri-la. A funny smile beams as he signals left, as jubilant as when Christopher Columbus landed in a new world.

"Francis, we're home." Alfred taps him on the shoulder to check on him.

Francis looks up and rubs his forehead where the medics placed the bandage.

"Wonderful. We made it in one piece. My Ferrari!" he exclaims after realizing what didn't make it.

"Looks like you'll just have to get a new one," says Alfred.

"I only got this one last month. Felicity helped pick it out," Francis says with a groan.

"Well, she can help you again."

Up in the distance, they can see Samuel perched on a swing made of an old tire and rope that hangs from a tree. Sanding material and paint cans are spread out on a tarp next to the front steps.

"That's right. It's time to treat the steps and balcony before the heavy autumn rains arrive and the leaves begin to fall from the trees," says Alfred with a grateful look in his eyes when he sees Samuel.

"Looks like Samuel started it for you," Francis points out, wagging a finger at the maintenance supplies askew on the ground.

"Yeah, Samuel's been doing a lot of the handiwork and upkeep on this place for years. I think he likes it here." Alfred smiles graciously.

Before Alfred parks the car, Samuel walks toward it, wearing a concerned smile, looking tired from worry. Approaching Alfred, he opens the car door, reaches in to grab his arm, and embraces him before he's completely out of the car.

"I'm all right, Samuel. It was a close call, but we're OK." Alfred returns the warm embrace. "Francis. Let's help Francis. Where's Felicity?"

"I sent her to take a walk on the beach and collect shells to decorate the dinner table tonight," Samuel says. "I'm making my specialty. She left just after you called. She should be back any moment now."

As Francis is about to exit the car, Samuel rushes over to help him out. "You've looked better," says Samuel, embracing Francis as well.

"Thank you. A bit of an adventure on the way in." Francis looks at the cracked windshield.

The three make their way to the house, stepping around the paint tins and other materials on the ground.

"Thanks again, Samuel. I'll give you a hand with this later," says Alfred, referring to the pile.

"You boys are lucky!" says Felicity as she comes around the corner, her pockets bulging with seashells. "How did you manage? I'd say you have lucky charms up your butts, both of you."

"Thank you, my love, that's lovely." Alfred smiles. "Come here."

Felicity approaches and wraps her arms around Alfred, squeezing him so tight, he can barely breathe.

"I'm all right, honey. Francis is a bit scratched up, but he'll survive as well," he whispers in her tight embrace.

Felicity stares intensely at Alfred, exhales, and starts to move to Francis.

Meow…meow…meow…

Felicity looks down at Alfred's coat. "What's this?" She pokes into his pocket.

"Oh, this is Matilda. I'll tell you all about her when we've settled back in the house. Let's wash up and have a big breakfast."

"Yo, cuz, come here and give us a hug. It will make me feel better," says Francis.

"Of course," says Felicity. She hugs Francis and then helps him up the stairs.

Samuel takes Alfred by the arm and helps him into the house as well.

"I'm all right, Samuel, no need to fuss," says Alfred, secretly enjoying his attention and affection.

"A telegram arrived for me this morning," announces Samuel.

"A telegram? Is that code for e-mail or a voice message?" asks Francis.

"No, a telegram. People still send them. Telegrams Canada, same-day delivery, and all that."

"OK. Where was it launched from, and from whom?" asks Alfred.

"Well, you see, that's the mysterious bit." Samuel removes the telegram from his pants pocket.

Alfred unfolds it and then looks at Samuel, surprised. "How can this be? I thought—"

"I know," Samuel interrupts.

"When?" asks Alfred.

"A week or so ago." Samuel takes the telegram from him and shoves it back into his pocket.

"Jack…Rose…Rose will be back in a week. They're both coming for the weekend," Alfred says excitedly. "I talked with Jack just before… he doesn't know anything about this."

"OK. Well, we can't do anything just now. Let's get you in the house and settled. We'll tell the others later."

"Of course. Certainly," agrees Alfred. Eager for a cup of coffee and a hot shower, he heads to the house.

Most anxious, most excited, and most unexpected, Samuel runs up behind Alfred.

"Rose," Samuel whispers to himself. "Rose," he whispers again. Then he stops cold in his tracks. Remembering the details of the event, he sits on a balcony chair, removes the telegram from his pocket, and reads it again.

> For five years I have prepared for this journey. Full stop. I've managed to find work on this cargo ship. Full stop. My escape was uneventful as they unlocked the prison doors and told me I was free to go. Full stop. I will see you soon. Full stop. Captain says we should arrive in seven days. Full stop. I have my visa. Full stop. Rose, of course. Full stop. Cherif. Full stop.

❖ ❖ ❖

It was June 2008, just before the rainy season in the Republic of Guinea. Samuel was joining Rose on an expedition project to track and document chimpanzees throughout the country. After months of exploration and thousands of hours of recording, Rose and Samuel had come to know many people and had developed close relationships with the women running an orphanage for children of all ages. They spent as many hours recording the women's work as they did the chimpanzees.

Aissatou and her husband, Bangoura, had started the orphanage after a major vehicle accident near their village, Moribadou, which had killed more than fifty people and left several babies and children without parents or families to care for them. Over the years, the orphanage had grown to house more than one hundred orphans and eight caregivers, all volunteers living on international aid and the goodwill of what people could share with them.

December 2008 brought the death of Guinea's national leader, Conté. Several hours after his death, Camara seized control in a coup, declaring himself head of the military junta. For months many protested against the coup, becoming violent and killing hundreds of people. In retaliation the junta ordered its soldiers to attack people who had protested against Camara as president. The soldiers went on a rampage, raping, mutilating, and murdering many innocent men, women, and children. Many, frightened for their lives, retaliated against one another, reporting secret hiding locations to save themselves and to win favor with the government. It was a total massacre. People fled for their lives, hiding anywhere they could, even in the forest.

Aissatou and her husband had to flee deep into the forest with all the children and the caregivers. Rose and Samuel followed suit, not wanting to abandon them in their time of need. After days in hiding, a military convoy approached. Soldiers spread out looking for them. The soldiers' mission was to eradicate the lot of them. Leaving burning villages and screams behind, the soldiers showed no mercy.

It was very early in the morning, just after sunrise. The babies were crying and hungry—twenty-eight in total. Each of the adults, including Rose and Samuel, and older children held a crying baby in his or her arms. The soldiers were approaching. The babies' cries were getting louder. Aissatou looked at everyone, gently placed her hand on her baby's face. Everyone holding a baby knew they had no choice but to do the same. Within moments the babies' cries stopped, and silence fell upon the hidden group as the soldiers walked past their prey. Cherif, Aissatou and Bangoura's fifteen-year-old son, was among the older children. After placing the dead baby on the wet ground, Cherif looked at his father and said he was going to look for food. Cherif never returned that day. They learned that the local police took him prisoner for stealing bread.

Cherif had been well educated by his parents, who had learned to speak English from missionaries. Cherif told the police that his name was Thomas, he was from Sierra Leone, and he spoke only English with little French. He pretended not to know the local language. They retained him for weeks. Then the local prefecture sent him to an unknown location for a few years, after which Cherif was transferred to Conakry. One morning the police went to Cherif's prison cell, opened the door, and told him he was free to go.

No one, not even Samuel, knew of Rose's true intentions when she returned to Guinea. All these years, they had stayed in contact with Aissatou and Bangoura, supporting their work to help the orphans.

How did Rose manage to find Cherif after all this time? Samuel wonders. Knowing Rose and her connections, it was possible. He always raised his hat to her for her inquisitive detective work.

"Samuel, breakfast is ready," shouts Felicity through the screen door. "Come before it gets cold."

Samuel looks up at her, his memories of Rose on hold. "I'll be right there, thank you."

Samuel and Rose had not seen each other since they returned from Guinea in 2009. Alfred didn't know the whole story. He just knew they had to go into hiding and of Cherif's disappearance; he never got the full story as to how they had gotten out alive.

Thou shalt not kill, Samuel remembered. *How many forms of mercy killing are there? Does God approve or object? What does the Bible say about killing the innocent to save the innocent?*

Be that as it may, Samuel made his choice that day, and he is prepared to answer for it. Returning the telegram to its safe haven in his pants pocket, he joins the others in the house for breakfast.

"Smells delicious. I hope we have lots of maple syrup," he says, taking his seat at the round kitchen table. "Today I'm making my specialty and will be sharing it with Mrs. Hitchcock, to thank her for her generosity. She's been sending freshly made baked goods to the house every day, and she's donating her time and all the bread, cakes, and anything else we need for Sunday's community theatrical performance, directed by Felicity's students, and the after-performance barbecue."

"I hear it's going to be a full house next weekend," says Francis as he sips his coffee.

"I received an e-mail from Rose with a letter addressed to all of you," says Felicity as she reaches for it on the kitchen counter. "She asked that I read it to all of you before she arrives next week. Don't all look so shocked. Rose and I have always stayed in touch. She's Luc's aunt, after all. But what I'm about to share with you is not about Luc. It's about someone she loved and didn't share with any of us, not even me. As usual, Rose asks for our forgiveness in advance—especially yours, Samuel. She hopes to appeal to our theatrical senses, the tragedian ways in which we live and have lived our lives. She sent the same letter to Jack. She figured we would have ample time to talk among ourselves before she arrives and never have to discuss it again. She fears that when she arrives, there may well be other matters to discuss, if Samuel hasn't already mentioned them, but she requests, if it's not too difficult for you," she says directly to Samuel, "to share them with us. Rose asks that you find the courage to do so. I've not read the letter yet. Rose asked that we all read it together."

Everyone is silent, perplexed, and waiting in anticipation as to what Felicity is about to read, and curious to hear what Samuel has to share.

Felicity takes a sip of tea, sits back in her chair, and addresses the group. "Please, keep eating as I read."

It was November 2000 when I got the news that I was accepted for my first long-awaited African assignment. I was overwhelmed with excitement when preparing for this trip. I could not stop thinking of the animals and what it would be like to be in Africa. I had thought this day would never come. Also, that summer was the first time Luc came to Africa. Felicity had been a few times before, and I looked forward to having them both with me. It was one of the best times of my life. Luc was thirteen and full of life. He couldn't get enough of the local music and dance moves.

That's also where Luc fell in love. His first love. Glory. I'll never forget her lovely little face. She was the youngest daughter of the village chief. By the way, I saw Glory a few weeks ago. She still wears the pendant Luc made for her. I thought you might like to know that, Felicity. I got off track a bit; let me get back to why I've written all of you.

However, to my surprise, my excitement of going to Africa was abruptly overshadowed by a strange dream one month before my scheduled departure. This dream turned my emotions upside down. The dream began in a Celtic setting. I was standing at the front entrance of my house, in the middle of a green field, facing a man on a horse. He was quite a long way away. The horse was facing the opposite direction, as if getting ready to leave. The man looked over at me. He was the love of my life, and he was leaving me because of a duty to marry someone else.

When I woke up, I realized that the message I had received was that I was going to meet the love of my life in Africa and have a relationship with him, but he would not be mine forever. The desire to meet this man was stronger than my initial reason to go to Africa. Because of this, I didn't know what to make of my vision, the message, and all the feelings that came with it. I was falling in love with someone I had never met.

Time sped by, and the next thing I knew, I was on a plane heading to Nigeria. After a few weeks of settling in, I was asked to give a lecture at a school in Port Harcourt about documenting wildlife. When the crew and I moved around in Nigeria, we sometimes traveled in luxury, thanks to one of the women on the conservation project whose husband just happened to be a chief pilot for a British helicopter company.

When I was on my way back from Port Harcourt, I met the man I had fallen in love with in my dream.

He was not on a horse, however, but in a car. I was waiting at the security gate of the helicopter compound when someone pointed him out to me and said, "That's who you are waiting for." The moment I saw him get out of his car, I knew this was the man I had seen in my dream. Not because of the way he looked, but because of the feelings I had and the energy I felt the moment I set eyes on him. We were introduced, and he said, "Nice to meet you" in his Welsh accent.

Could my dream have been any clearer? I thought.

A few days after being back at our compound, a pilot friend told me that this man, William, had asked about me. William then called me, asking all sorts of technical questions about a flight he was doing for another documentary. I knew he was looking for a reason to call me because I definitely was not the person he should have been talking to. He invited my colleagues and me to a weekend event called a "hash." A hash is a disorganized race where people do stupid things and wear the stupidest costumes while running for miles. There's also lots of drinking during and after the race. I was not the least bit interested in this, but it was a good excuse to get away for the weekend and get to know William.

The weekend arrived, and on the first night, William and I talked about many things, including his being a married man. He told me he wanted to meet me. He said he didn't really like the hash but figured it was an excuse to get me out to Eket, where he was stationed. I told him I didn't get involved with married men. We still spent the entire weekend together, having fun. I wasn't sure what I felt at the time. I was confused about being in love with someone I had never met, yet there he was, a married man, completely unavailable in the truest sense.

However, a couple of months later, I went against everything I believed in and started an affair with him. We got on very well and loved each other, but I knew the inevitable was going to happen: I would leave the project in Nigeria, and he would return to his life with his wife and children in Wales without me. It was extremely painful to walk away from him, but I knew it had to be done. We had lots of fun when we were together, and we had become very good friends.

A year after being back in Canada, I was contacted to work in Mauritania. I was very excited and looked forward to returning to Africa, especially to a country that was part of the Sahara. I had also found out that William was going to be there. Shooting the documentary required plenty of air travel around the desert and over the sea. My contract was for six months, and I was looking forward to everything that waited for me there. I had hoped that Luc could come to Mauritania as well. He turned out to be a great field research assistant. He also always talked about how much he wanted to experience trekking throughout the desert on camelback and camping in remote places where he could explore ancient ruins. But he wasn't feeling well that year. It was shortly after I returned to Canada that he was diagnosed with cancer.

William arrived three weeks after I did. In the meantime I flew to Perth to meet the Australian crew on this joint documentary project. I didn't know what it would be like when I saw William and what would happen when we were together every day for six months. Again, it was exactly as my vision had predicted. William was flying a helicopter from England, and the day he landed, I felt very calm. Within a week we were back in bed and spent every night together, eating every meal together, until it was time for us to part again. This time it was even more painful than the last, but we both knew it had to be this way. We really enjoyed each other. We made love on the beach and in the pool and would disappear at lunch to make love again. The Islamic Republic of Mauritania never missed a prayer. Before sunrise a prayer always echoed through Nouakchott. For us, it was lovemaking time.

Despite my visions foretelling the outcome of this affair, I went ahead, throwing all I had into it, even though I knew William would never leave his wife and family. He loved them too much. Oddly enough, I also didn't want him to leave them. He never would have stayed with me because he could not live without them.

When we parted, it was an extremely painful separation. I couldn't stop crying. I would scream into my pillow at night because I missed him so much. Eventually, these fits of pain and sorrow subsided, and I began to feel more at ease with my life and our friendship. I was staying in England with friends after my contract in Mauritania. William and I were still talking every day, and we decided I would visit him in Nigeria. I did that twice. One morning, during my second visit, while he was getting ready for work, he asked if I could bring some more wine and cheese on my next visit.

I promised that I would, but in that same moment, I knew there would not be a third time. I was sitting partially up in bed, watching him get dressed, when suddenly a message came in. I didn't want to believe it. The message was like one of those signs hanging in a motel window, flashing "No Vacancies" in bright red, but this sign read, "No, you won't be back, and you will never see him again."

What else could I do but nod in agreement and say I would bring some wine and cheese? That was spring 2004, and I have not seen him in the flesh since. It is now 2014. It wasn't until December 2013 that I was able to find the courage and strength to break all communication with him.

My ghosts, however, do not end there. Samuel, I hope you can forgive me. "Tragedy of the moth" is how I once described myself. Before I knew I was going on assignment to Nigeria, I decided to move to Whistler for a bit of R and R. I wanted to take in the sights and do a bit of hiking and cross-country skiing. However, while in Whistler, I reconnected with my friend Wayne. Wayne and I had been casual lovers since I was eighteen. Wayne and I had talked often about our relationship; I always wanted more, but Wayne never believed he would be enough for me. We led very different lives, and Wayne believed I was always on one adventure or another. But we always remained friends. I once confessed to him that one of my concerns while I was in Whistler was that I would see him out on a date with someone else, and that would be difficult for me. Wayne was not faithful in his relationships, so I asked him to never make me part of his cheating. I asked that he always tell me if he was in a relationship because I would never sleep with him while he was involved with someone else. That was before William, of course. Samuel, I hope you are still with everyone while Felicity reads this letter.

One night, Wayne invited me over for dinner. I knew it was an invitation to spend the night. While sitting on the sofa, drinking red wine, which was one of our favorite things to do, we talked about a print hanging on his living-room wall. The print was of bears in a circle, dancing. I asked that he leave the print to me if he should die. He agreed. I didn't know then that this would be the last time I would ever see him. He was about to die. That night we made love for the last time. I didn't spend the night, though. I left because Wayne confessed that he was dating someone else. Of course, I was very angry, hurt, and disappointed. He had known that I never wanted to be part of something like that. Wayne was very upset that I was so upset. When I left his room, he reached his hand out to me while he was still lying back, but I just walked away. I never saw or spoke to him after that; I only wrote him a letter once I was in Nigeria.

"More coffee, anyone?" asks Francis as he fills his cup.

"Yes, please." Felicity slides her cup closer to Francis. Samuel is silent.

"Samuel, coffee, tea, anything?" Francis taps his cup with the coffeepot. Felicity continued reading.

Part of my maturing, even in my thirties and early forties, involved understanding what it meant to have wisdom. Through some of my trials in life, I felt as if I had lost my soul and could not find my way. I wanted to know all the answers to my life and what I needed to do to make myself different so I could move on and realize my dreams. I had been seeking love, family, and a career that would bring me joy every day. I felt it was nothing special, but something most people wanted in their lives.

So one day, I asked for wisdom. I thought this request was going to be an easy journey, a ticket to my own salvation, a road map to my dreams and life's purpose. Well, I couldn't have been more wrong. It was the most difficult and challenging ten years of my life. There was no peace, no joy, and no happiness attached to this journey. What I was given were opportunities to help me realize my own potential, my own dreams, and my life's purpose and to see who I really was. I didn't realize this early on in the journey because I was still too naive and hurt and was a victim of life's circumstances. It was a hard lesson to learn, but looking back, I wouldn't have changed anything. All the experiences I had through the choices I made brought me to where I am today. The gift of knowing who you are is a gift beyond words. It is my life's purpose to understand and accept the responsibility of living. And for much of this, I have Luc to thank. Through his wisdom and courage, he showed me how his choice to die was out of his own courage to live a life free of regret, of unwanted and unnecessary pain and sorrow. Luc and I spent hours talking, especially in his last six months. He was keen to join the afterlife just so he could get on with life.

As I was saying, I was on a quest for wisdom, and thanks to this, despite the outcome, the pain and the sorrow from my very brief marriage, I would not have changed the course of the events that led me to my ex-husband. Yes, Samuel, I was married once. I was in my twenties. I was married to my childhood friend, Troy, who completely screwed it up by taking his shit out on me. I was heartbroken and felt betrayed by him. I had never believed he would hit me. I was even more heartbroken when I lost the baby. The week I married, I learned that I was pregnant, but I later had a miscarriage. Troy focused only on himself throughout all of this. He could not get past his own pain. Troy hurt me deeply, and it took me years to be rid of the pain. But because of my experience with him, I am now awake.

I have reached a level of awareness and consciousness I hadn't even known existed. This self-awareness and consciousness didn't make my life any easier. It was the beginning of my life, and that was when the real hard work started.

I discussed all of this with Luc during his last few weeks. He asked to meet me one day. Felicity, you were out. It was the afternoon you asked me to sit with him while you went out to get medical supplies. Luc was keen to know and learn more about other people's struggles. I guess he figured I was a big enough mess to be an excellent case study. Despite my own struggles, I continued with my desire to achieve my dreams and reach for my goals. Looking forward required that I take a good look back to make sure I wasn't repeating choices that were not right for me, not in line with my intuition, my gut, my soul. However, without being terribly hard on ourselves, I'm sure we can all look at moments in our lives and say, "What the fuck was I thinking?"

Everyone but Samuel laughed. "I'm quite impressed with our little Rose," says Alfred as Samuel starts to clear the plates from the table.

"Not so fast, my love," says Felicity as she turns the pages of the letter. "There's more." Samuel places the plates on the kitchen counter and sits back at the table.

One day Luc asked me about Buddhism. So I shared with him what I had learned throughout the years and gave him a few books to read. I explained to Luc that I, in various ways, was discovering who I was. Through this internal journey, I learned that honoring myself began with accountability. The new Rose had no room for a sense of entitlement. I had to go after what I wanted in life, and that included peace of mind. I had no idea how I was going to achieve this. All I could do was ask for it and trust that I was on the right path and that I would get to where I wanted to be." Last stop, peace of mind," I would say. Peace of mind, body, and soul is what Luc yearned for. He was desperate during those last few weeks. Through a multitude of books and meeting like-minded people, I continued to learn. I was still stubborn and resisted the obvious. I struggled with the desire to get what I wanted and ignored my intuition. After a few years, I became tired of fighting with myself and started to have the courage to trust myself and believe in myself and my own intuition.

When I left Mauritania, I stayed with friends in England. One day I couldn't get Wayne out of my mind. I could feel his energy; it was very strong. I wanted to call him and see how he was because I usually knew when something was wrong with him. Since I had known him, I had visions or messages in my dreams about him. When I had these visions, I would call him the next day, and Wayne would validate what I was sensing. But this time I decided not to call him. On that January day, I made the decision that we both had to move on with our lives after that last night we had spent together in Whistler. Later that year I was back in Canada, and I decided to take a few weeks off in Nova Scotia. I spent one day at the Mi'kmaq reserve to learn about the community and culture. One day when I was in the community center, I started to smell the soap that Wayne always used. I wondered if he was trying to contact me because the night before, I had had a terrible dream about him. He had been standing with two boys, one on each side of him. They had very sad faces, and the energy was depressing and worrisome. They were not happy in the dream. I didn't understand this vision. The only thing I could think of at the time was when his ex-girlfriend had had an abortion without telling him. He had found out in a most unpleasant way. I had seen the death of his child through a dream. He had been holding a child and crying. I had called him the next day, and he'd told me he had just found out about the abortion. His girlfriend had gone through with the procedure without telling him.

At the community center, Wayne's energy continued to get stronger and stronger. The next morning I decided to call him. However, before someone answered the phone, I knew that whoever answered would tell me that he had died. It was now September 2004, and I had *just learned that my lover of fifteen years had died that January. No one had contacted me because his family didn't know how to reach me. I then spoke with his brother, and he informed me that Wayne had died in a skiing accident. He had been in a new relationship and had a six-month-old son. I was devastated. The only saving grace I could see in all of this was that we weren't together. I doubt I could have survived this loss. When I returned to Vancouver, Wayne's brother sent me a copy of the CD that was shown at his memorial service. I printed a photo of Wayne holding his son. To this day I still have that photo on my bookshelf. Luc was intrigued and fascinated with this story. He told me that he would come see me once he crossed over and tell me all the secrets of the afterlife.*

"I wondered whose photo that was. I never asked. She must have been so heartbroken. She never mentioned this or shared her suffering with anyone," says Alfred, looking over at Samuel, who was sitting quietly, taking all this in.

"She never did and never does," agreed Felicity.

Since that first contact with Wayne, I have felt him with me. As strange as this may sound, Wayne and I have become friends like I never could have imagined, and I'm extremely grateful for this. Later that fall, I heard Wayne say, "Rose, it's time you went to see where I'm buried. You need to do this so you can move on from all of this." It was a Sunday morning. I called the Capilano View Cemetery to find out where he was buried. It was a big place, and I had never been there. The office was closed, so I said to Wayne, "I can go today, but you'll need to be very clear on the directions once I get there." Wayne provided the exact location: "When you get there, turn right and turn right again. Walk a bit to your left near the end, and I'll be there."

Again, as strange as talking to a "ghost" sounds, I trusted what I was hearing, so I got in the car and drove to the cemetery. When I arrived, I followed the instructions and parked the car. I sat there for a moment, looking around. I felt empty and hollow. I stepped out of the car and walked in the direction Wayne had instructed, which was directly in front of me and to the left. I walked with my head down, reading the names on the tombstones. Within a few seconds, I found myself looking down at Wayne's grave. I fell to my knees; I was crying and couldn't stop. I lay next to him for quite a while, staring at the grass. I kept reading his name, engraved in the dark headstone, flat against the ground, over and over again. I couldn't believe my eyes. I couldn't believe my friend was dead and buried under my feet. I was also surprised that he could communicate so clearly with me. It was time for me to leave. I returned only one other time, on Christmas Day that year, to place a rose on his grave.

What the heart can feel when left alone,
Alone to live,
Alone to love,
Alone to grieve.
Standing still by his grave,
His body still,

I kneel to him,
Hand on heart.
The Earth is still.

He lies below
Yet stands with me.
His spirit near,
He hears my tears.

Can I leave him,
This man so dear?
Where do I go,
And how do I live?

How does this journey end?
When love is lost
Through death and sorrow,
Where do we go?

Come back, my friend.
Why did you go?
Your life was young,
With dreams to follow.

A shadow appears
Next to my soul.
My love is near.
Never shall I go.

I will be coming home now.

Love,
R.

PS. Samuel, like Luc, you and I and everyone that day made the right choice. We can honor those babies' memories by living our lives.

Felicity wipes her tears. She gazes deeply into Alfred's eyes and says, "My love, Rose is truly alive."

Even Alfred's eyes are a bit misty, and he squeezes her hand in comfort. Francis wipes his tears. All three look over at Samuel, who is still extremely silent and still. He releases a tear.

"More and more, I'm beginning to understand why Jack has been so protective of his little sister. Eliot must be looking forward to seeing her again as well."

"Well, I just want her home safe and sound," declares Samuel, pushing his plate away.

"Would you like some more?" asks Alfred.

"Of course, thank you. More of that crispy bacon would be nice."

"You all right, Samuel?" asks Felicity as she pours him another cup of coffee.

"I'm curious," says Francis. "After all that, what's the story Rose wishes for you to share with us? Since we're all here, you might as well tell us. Why stop here?"

Alfred turns toward Samuel with a look of apprehension as he places a full plate in front of Samuel.

"Thanks, Alfred," Samuel says, ignoring Francis. He eats everything on his plate until there's nothing left. The others wait and watch with anticipation.

"More, Samuel?" asks Felicity.

"No, thank you," replies Samuel, followed by a big sip of coffee. Then he takes the telegram out of his pocket and places it on the table.

"I received a telegram today. Rose didn't go to Guinea only to shoot a documentary. She also went to help a friend."

"What do you mean?" asks Felicity, intrigued with curiousity, elbow on table, chin resting in the palm of her hand. "She didn't mention any of this in her e-mails. I hope she's OK."

"Yes, she's OK. What I'm about to share with you, we have never shared with anyone before, not even you, Alfred." Samuel looks pensively at him. Playing with his fork, scraping an empty plate, he looks at all of them. "Rose and I…we…us…the young man who's meeting us in a week—"

"What young man?" interrupts Felicity.

"The young man who Rose…" Unable to speak without choking up and crying, he pauses to take a deep breath. "When Felicity and I were in Nigeria together, we…we…committed a most unconscionable act. There were twenty-eight babies…"

❖ ❖ ❖

Moral consciousness, obligation, choices, actions taken to rise above an obstacle rather than to fall victim, in order to maintain a marvelous hold on life, are the reasoning. How inadequate, choosing in the face of terror, ignorance, vengeance, regret, honor. What capacity for suffering can one person sustain except the will to be strong, to shoulder the unforgivable, to avoid being vague, but to decide and commit? Movement of unusual energy pulling in all directions and speaking out loud of unconventional woes of human form. Rivals wielding their swords, tempting the soft, mild voice to come forth with an appetite to neither accept nor refuse but to ravage. Both sinister and transcendent is the profound prolonging to explore the extent by which intimacy of the soul resists the irresistible and embraces all offensives. Escape is never an option. In an attempt to forgive our offenses by rubbing out the stain on our flesh, tragicomedy sneaks in, challenging pejorative minds.

The Best Look at Yourself

Watching what was,
A figure appears.
A mirror reflection of the soul's appeal.

A chance to see.
A chance to greet.
A chance to be

Here with thee.
A balance beam.
A reflection appears.

A closer look.
A frown,
A smirk.
What do you see?

An opportunity to be.

"Samuel, help clean up the kitchen so Alfred and Francis may get cleaned up before taking a rest. They've been through quite a bit this morning," directs Felicity as she begins to clear the table. Then she mutters, "All those years, what do you know? Rose had a secret lover."

"I'm shocked," replies Francis, overhearing her. "I thought she just didn't want to be with me."

"She doesn't want to be with you even when she's single," replies Felicity. "You're not her type."

"What do you mean I'm not her type? I'm handsome, rich, and creative. I'm not like those rich, boring businessmen," replies Francis, stroking his hair. Everyone bursts into hysterical laughter, completely out of control.

Samuel raps the kitchen table sharply, startling everyone. They all stare at him, and he boldly stands from his chair.

"The burden—" he starts.

"Remorse is not an option, Samuel," Felicity interrupts, taking away his dirty plate. "Instead, help Francis to his room, run him a bath, and make sure he doesn't slip and smack his head. Your consciousness is intact, Samuel. So is Rose's, and so are all the others'."

"I'll clean up here with Felicity, and then I think I'm going to make love to my beautiful huldra, so, Samuel, please do not bother me for the rest of the afternoon," teases Alfred.

"I'll be with Mrs. Hitchcock," replies Samuel. "Once I get Francis sorted, I'll cook up a storm and bring some to Hitchcock Buns as a test run, to see if it's to her satisfaction. I'll be back for dinner tonight."

"Oh, that reminds me, Felicity," says Alfred. "When I saw Mrs. Hitchcock at the gas station, she gave me a parcel to give to you. She said it's something she found at her sister's house while sorting out her affairs."

Alfred walks to the coffee table in the living room, a very open space, while Felicity watches with great curiosity, wondering what the parcel could be.

"Here you go." Alfred hands her a beautifully wrapped package with a white-rose ribbon and a "Hitchcock Buns" label. Everyone, equally curious, watches as Felicity unwraps her mysterious parcel. A heavy silence falls upon her as the item is revealed.

"Well, what is it?" asks Samuel impatiently. "The suspense is killing us."

"There's a note with it," says Felicity.

Dear Felicity,

It is with great joy that I give you this wonderful photograph of you and Luc taken a year before he was taken sick.

God bless,
Mrs. H

"How did she know that this is Luc and that it was a year before he died?" asks Felicity. "I forgot about that day. It's a beautiful photo of Luc."

Alfred takes it from her. "Yes, it's beautiful. You're lucky to have this. It was very considerate of Mrs. Hitchcock."

"Yes, but how did she know?" insists Felicity.

"What does it matter?" replies Samuel. "Don't look at me. I never met him, so how could I know it was a year before—"

"Hmmm." Felicity takes the photo from Alfred to show Francis.

"I've seen this photo before, Felicity," he says, sounding perplexed and curious.

"What do you mean? How's that possible?" She takes the photo from him, fixated, unable to take her eyes away from Luc.

"The book *The Works of Martha Wilson* was published just before she died. Mother has a copy of it. Didn't you know about the book, Felicity?" Francis asks.

"No. Yes. I forgot."

Alfred takes the photo from her. "Let's place it over there, on top of the fireplace. A portrait," he says, smiling. "Martha's photographic work can be enjoyed, a memory ready to be appreciated from a different standpoint in the sense of visual pleasure, Luc's wise face a vessel of untapped emotions. The raven that flew solo withheld in midflight, Christian laws broken, sheltered by his mother, bound by infinite affection. Is there such a thing as a virtuous sin? Man would call this a debt to be paid, and neither the sinner nor the beggar ever would owe."

"For the love of God, what are you going on about, Alfred?" Samuel grabs the photo from him, walks to the fireplace, and places it to the left. "There. Perfect. Now we can all enjoy it anytime."

"I'm just saying that history shows, and I have it on high authority, that our worst enemy can be ourselves. I always figured you a saint, Samuel, and you still are, in my eyes. But in others I don't think so because, well…" Alfred's diatribe trails off as he focuses on a tiny piece of wiggling fur. "Matilda. There she is. Come, Matilda."

"Necessary evil. There's a play for you. How many times has something like this been written? I've always believed that art imitates life. Never has it been the other way around," Samuel says, and then he walks to the kitchen, removes the necessary ingredients from the refrigerator, and slams the cold fish onto the counter. "And you, Francis, you're just there, writing about your fucking horse in the sky. Now tell me—what the fuck is that about?"

Startled by Samuel's frankness, Francis says defensively, "Hey, wait a minute. How did I get into this? And what do you mean, my fucking horse in the sky?"

Samuel waves his cold, dead fish in the air. "Yes, Felicity told me all about your little play, which she thinks is brilliant by the way, but really, come on. His entire life is fucking wasted, passed right before his eyes. What a stupid kid."

"Why? Did it strike a nerve, Samuel?" Francis bites back and gets up from the table. "Time for my bath, which you're supposed to help me with so I don't slip and crack my head, remember?"

Samuel puts the fish back on the counter; covers it with a wet, cool cloth, and says, "I'll be right back, Mr. Fish."

"Only a week to go, Samuel, before you see her again," says Francis. "She didn't waste her life."

"Sir Francis, let me run you a bath," says Samuel. He helps Francis from the table and walks off, leaving Felicity and Alfred with Matilda.

7

Early morning. Day of the community festival. Last outdoor theater production of the season. The beach house yard covered with orange, red, and yellow leaves. The waves crashing on the beach. Salmon hanging in the smokehouse at the back of the house. Cut wood piled at the corner of the house, next to the porch. Wind chimes singing in the wind. Seals on the rocks near the beach house. People walking on the beach, some playing with their kites. Dogs playing on the beach. Seabirds flying around and squawking, collecting mussels, dropping them on the rocks. Felicity's students rehearsing lines on the beach.

JUSTIN: Try again, and this time slower.

ARNOLD: (*Scruffy hair, comedic characteristics; wiggles his ass, speaks slowly. The others watch with laughter.*) What, you want me to do it his way?

SABRINA: You are the master. I salute you!

JASON: Don't listen to him.

ARNOLD: (*Stays in character. Dances around the others, chanting and grinning.*) I am a fool!

JUSTIN, JASON, SABRINA: Bravo! Bravo! Bravo!

ARNOLD: (*Takes a bow, bends like a fool.*) Until next time.

Exits the makeshift stage made of rocks. Removes his shoes and socks and runs to the water, jumping in and out. Laughing out loud, running up and down the beach. Dead seagull on the beach; he crouches to observe, covers it with sand, and draws a cross in the sand next to it. The sound of slap, slap, slap, slap in the water—a large tail pounds the sea and dives back under the water. Eyes peer to see in the distance, the reflection of the sun blinding. A kite escapes. A dog chases it; a boy chases the dog; the father chases the boy. Arnold dives for the kite string in the sand, knocking over the dog. All's well—kite recovered. A seagull shits on his head. Laughter from a distance. He kneels in the sand, bent over, to rinse the shit from his hair. More laughter in the background. From the corner of his eye, he sees the dog running back. It mounts him from behind and humps. Hysterical laughter all around. He pushes the dog away gently, pats him on the head, and shoos him away. The others come to his aid, laughing.

SABRINA: A Conversation

When a conversation begins, a window of opportunity
for a friendship appears
A friendship started, longed for
The beginning of a new journey
A path of discovery
A place to be
A moment to embrace
A journey begins with a new, shining star
A direction you want to follow
A place to see
The explorer finds a map
Picks a spot
Compass pointed, the walk begins
On this path she meets a guide
Not what she expected, but she's pleased with him
She likes this guide

A teacher, a student, a friend
One entity, one soul, one memory, one place
A conversation begins
And words are shared
Life is shared

ARNOLD: You remembered. Fantastic!

SABRINA: I was laughing so much, it just came out. Thank you!

Hugs him. They all embrace and walk arm in arm on the beach. The sun is still low in the sky. They watch the seals slide back into the sea. The sound of slaps against the sea turns their heads. A distance away, a whale awaits.

JUSTIN: Let's get our kayaks. We still have time.

JASON: Three hours. Plenty of time.

They run to the house. Felicity is outside raking leaves. The students arrive to collect the kayaks hung in the boat shed. Excitedly, they get their gear and head off to the sea. Felicity rejoices in their joy.

FELICITY: Have fun! (*Waves.*)

SAMUEL: (*Comes out of smokehouse, still in pajamas, cheerful.*) The kids? Lovely day for kayaking.

FELICITY: (*Places rake on the ground and picks up big, black garbage bag.*) Come here, please. Can you hold this while I collect the leaves?

SAMUEL: My pleasure. (*Takes the bag, stands motionless, watching her every move, wondering what more she knows about Rose. Hesitant.*) So tell me. Rose…

FELICITY: (*Stuffs the bag with leaves, pressing down, taking a moment.*) Pejorative behavior isn't part of this discussion. It cannot be part of this at all.

SAMUEL: (*Curious, uncertain, helps her fill the bag with leaves.*) Of course not! And saying that means…Did you say "pejorative"? I haven't heard anyone use that word in a long time. You have my undivided attention, Felicity! Once we're done here, I'd like to hear everything you have to say. Yesterday was enlightening, to say the least. Pejorative! I'm the last one ever to be such. Rose and I will have lots to answer for one day, I'm sure—maybe. We are haunted by guiltless feelings at times and tormented with guilt at the same time. These ghosts will be with us forever.

Felicity rakes more leaves into a pile. Reflects on her choices of words. Keeps her head down as she continues raking. She looks up suddenly at a crackling sound coming from the forest. A black bear strolls among the trees. She signals to Samuel to look behind him. They both stand still, watching for what the bear will decide to do. She remembers telling both Samuel and Alfred that the smokehouse would attract bears, but Samuel was determined to smoke his own salmon for this festival. Samuel scratches his head, looking cautiously at the bear. It stops and looks around, sniffing in their direction. The bear sits and watches them. No one is moving.

SAMUEL: (*Whispering.*) Felicity. Felicity, what do you want to do?

FELICITY: Don't move. Just be quiet.

SAMUEL: Yeah, but do I just stand here?

FELICITY: Yes, just watch. But if you must, slowly step backward. Don't turn your back to him. Walk back slowly toward me.

Samuel slowly takes a step back. The bear gets up from its seated position. Stares at Samuel. Samuel freezes and waits to see the bear's next move before taking another step. The bear lifts his nose, sniffing the air. Samuel thinks it was a bad idea to have the smokehouse so close to the house without a fence. He takes another slow step backward. The bear starts walking toward them. The bear stops, his head partially out of the forest line into the backyard.

SAMUEL: (*Anxious, loud whisper.*) Fuck! Felicity! He's coming this way.

FELICITY: I can see that. Let's wait one more moment to see what he does.

SAMUEL: And then what?

FELICITY: I don't know. (*She looks around. The porch is too far. Bear spray and horn are on the porch, hanging near the door.* Fuck, *she thinks. The bear moves toward them with a few more steps. Felicity shouts.*) Hey! Go away! (*The bear stops, turns around, and walks the other way, back into the forest. Felicity and Samuel stand there, startled.*)

SAMUEL: Is that all it took?

FELICITY: I'm not sure, but I think we're lucky on this one. Come here; let's finish this up. Then we'll take a long walk on the beach, and I'll tell you all about your Rose. You will love her more, Samuel.

SAMUEL: Love?

FELICITY: (*Looks at him, frowning.*) Can we just get this done? We don't have all day.

Samuel hurries up, anxious to get this done and get on with the walk. They fill the bags with leaves and put the rakes put back in the shed. Alfred is still sleeping. Felicity leaves a note for him on the kitchen table: "8:00 a.m. Gone for a walk with Samuel. Back around 10:00. XX, F." She and Samuel walk along the beach, away from the kids playing with their kites. They scramble back and forth to avoid letting the waves reach their feet. They see a whale in the distance and watch it for a while. The waves crash along the cliff up ahead, making a pounding noise, drawing everyone's attention.

Birds fly off the cliff face, just above the splashing waves. Tripping over the seaweed carried in by the waves, Samuel untangles it from his feet. Felicity holds him up to keep him steady as the waves crash onto the beach. Samuel gives in to the waves—he removes his shoes, rolls up his pants, and jumps into the water up to his knees. He laughs and runs up and down the beach. Felicity watches with laughter. She runs to reach him and helps him out of the water. They find a nook on the beach, far in enough so the waves can't reach them, with a perfect view. Samuel dries his feet with his shirt. They sit quietly for a few minutes. Felicity sits back, resting against a driftwood log. From her eyes, Samuel knows she's about to tell the tale of his beloved Rose.

❖ ❖ ❖

ALFRED: (*Stretching and yawning, looks out the window.*) What a beautiful day.

He gets out of bed and goes to the toilet for a long-needed piss. After the last shake, he wanders to the sink to wash his hands. He takes a long look in the mirror. Greets himself. Rubs his bristly face. Looks down at the electric razor. Not charged. Plugs it in. Goes to the kitchen, searching for a cup of coffee. Sees the note on the kitchen table. Looks up at the clock—8:20 a.m. With enough time to spare, he decides to spend a bit catching up with the Magdalene. *She's been docked for two weeks—the longest it's been since he's taken her out. On his way to the boat, his phone rings.*

ALFRED: Good morning, good people. Lovely day today.

MARGARET: Good morning to you too, Alfred.

ALFRED: Mrs. Warthog, lovely to hear your voice. When will we have the pleasure of your company?

MARGARET: Well, since it's a lovely day, we were thinking of arriving a bit early. I know the festivities don't begin until later this afternoon and usually last way into the evening, but it's too nice to come later.

ALFRED: No problem. Come on by anytime. When should we expect you?

MARGARET: Eliot and I decided to get an early start on the weekend. We arrived Thursday. Last night, the sea was calm. It was a lovely night to cross over. We're staying in that beautiful B and B just up from the Hitchcock Buns bakery, so we're not that far away. We were thinking around elevenish?

ALFRED: Great. See you then.

MARGARET: Alfred?

ALFRED: Yes, Margaret.

MARGARET: Our daughter, Georgette, is back from Africa. She and Rose caught up over there.

ALFRED: Oh yeah?

MARGARET: Yes. She met up with Rose in Guinea, and because of the ebola outbreak and some other urgent matter, she decided to come back home, so she says.

ALFRED: I see. Do you know what urgent matter she's referring to? Is Georgette well?

MARGARET: Yes, she's fine. No, I don't know which urgent matter she's referring to. She just said there's someone she wants us to meet, and she said he would be at your place this weekend.

ALFRED: I see.

MARGARET: Do you know who she's referring to, Alfred?

ALFRED: (*Suspecting he knows who it might be.*) No, Margaret, I don't. I'm curious as well. I just know we'll be meeting some new people this weekend. It's always the case during the festival weekend.

MARGARET: Yes, you're right. See you later. Good-bye for now.

ALFRED: Good-bye. (*He stares at the phone. Talks to himself, wondering what the weekend will be like with all these characters in the same place. Happy to arrive at the pier where the* Magdalene *waits for him.*)

ARNOLD: Alfred! (*Waves. Walks up on the pier with Jason in tow.*)

ALFRED: Hello! (*Surprised to see them there. He was so much looking forward to a bit of alone time with the* Magdalene.)

ARNOLD: Hi! Arnold. (*Pointing at himself.*) Jason. (*He points to Jason, who waves.*)

ALFRED: Yes, I remember. How are you? Where are the others? Felicity said some of you would be by very early this morning.

ARNOLD: Yeah, that's Sabrina and Justin. Figured we'd give them some alone time. We happened to be walking by and saw you.

ALFRED: That's very considerate. What are you boys up to?

ARNOLD: Nothing much. We just thought we'd walk around and check out the place.

ALFRED: Well, you're in the right place. There's a lot to see. (*He steps onto the fifty-foot sailboat, which he feels he's completely abandoned these past couple of weeks.*)

ARNOLD: We were thinking maybe we can hang with you for a bit. We'd love to see your boat. Permission to come aboard, Captain?

ALFRED: Of course. Let me give you a hand. (*He smiles at the boys and puts out his hand to help them onto the boat. Jason, clumsy by nature, trips.*) Watch your step.

JASON: Thank you. She's a beaut, Mr. Manning.

ALFRED: Thank you. Alfred. You can call me Alfred.

JASON: Sure.

ALFRED: You boys know how to sail?

JASON and ARNOLD: (*Speak at the same time.*) Yeah!

JASON: We've been taking lessons at the sailing school just up from the theater. But I've never sailed anything like this.

ALFRED: Would you like to? I need to take her out, stretch her legs. She's been neglected.

JASON and ARNOLD: (*Speak at the same time.*) Awesome!

ARNOLD: What do you want us to do?

ALFRED: Let's begin by untying those ropes, and then come here and we'll begin. Short trip—we need to be back by ten.

Alfred gives them a quick tour of the boat and tells them about the ins and outs of this and that. They're off. Wind in their hair, the guys have embarked on a short yet incredible journey on the Magdalene, *which they've heard so much about. They sail up the coastline, waves pounding the boat. Everyone cheers with joy. The sails are up. The sound of their flapping echoes the voice of freedom. All three are in absolute ecstasy from the salt water drying on their lips. They see Felicity and Samuel sitting on the beach. They wave. Felicity and Samuel stand, waving back at the guys.*

FELICITY: (*Brushes the sand from her pants and does the same to Samuel.*) We should be heading back. By the time we get home, they'll be coming in.

SAMUEL: Thank you for telling me a bit more about Rose. I understand now.

FELICITY: (*Giggling, taking him by the arm.*) Good. Maybe now you can move out like a big boy and make a home of your own.

SAMUEL: There's a thought. But I'll miss you guys. (*He puts his arm around Felicity, and they walk back slowly, enjoying the view.*) Thank you. (*He kisses her on the head.*)

The morning drifts slowly and calmly. They walk home in silence. Samuel stares at the sea the entire way. His breath is shallow and slow. Felicity remains close to him, guiding him as he unknowingly drifts toward the water.

SAMUEL: Felicity, I know it is still difficult for you to talk about Luc and those last days. I just want to say for the record that I've only had nothing but great respect and admiration for what you did for Luc. I can only imagine how difficult it must have been for you. I'm sure there are no words to describe those last moments. (*Felicity walks arm in arm with Samuel and tells him of those last moments with Luc.*)

After swallowing the overdose of medication, Luc smiled at Felicity with peace and gratitude in his eyes. She turned off all the machines. Silence filled the room. A peacefulness not felt for a very long time by both of them filled the space. Felicity lay next to Luc on the bed, placing his head on her shoulder, caressing him. They looked into each other's eyes, quiet, feeling only each other's breath until Luc's eyes closed. His breathing was shallow. His body jerked, struggling through his last few breaths. Silence. His body was still.

SABRINA: Felicity, hi! (*Waving her arms.*)

FELICITY: Hi, Sabrina. (*Waving back. Wiping her tears. Samuel holding her tightly.*)

JUSTIN: (*Hand in hand with Sabrina; he runs to Felicity and Samuel.*) Hi. Hope we're not intruding. Wasn't expecting to see you on the beach this morning. We decided to get an early start with our final rehearsal before tonight's performance.

FELICITY: No, it's fine. You both know Samuel.

JUSTIN and SABRINA: (*Speak at the same time.*) Yes, we remember Samuel. Nice to see you again.

SAMUEL: (*Speaking slowly, snapping out of his all-consuming thoughts.*) Nice to see you as well. I look forward to the performance tonight. I hear you've all worked extremely hard. There's always a great reward for that.

Felicity looks at him, perplexed and with admiration as she sees something in him she has never seen or known before. He is freeing his heart from the sadness he has held for so many years.

FELICITY: Will you come to the house with us now or join us later?

SABRINA: No, we'll stay here for a while longer and enjoy this beautiful morning. We saw some of the guys with Alfred on the boat. Looks like they were having lots of fun. You think they'll come back?

They all look out in the distance at the guys on the boat. Laughter.

FELICITY: I'm not sure.

SAMUEL: It looks like they're on their way to Lighthouse Point. Did you know that on the other side of the point is the oldest house on the island? It was built in 1890 by a French settler who heard of this beautiful place. He couldn't imagine that a place like this could exist, so he set off one day from his small village in France with only the clothes on his back, earning his way with all sorts of jobs. When he arrived in Ontario, he met a beautiful Algonquin Indian woman. It was love at first sight. Eventually her father blessed the union, and the two continued on this journey together, arriving over there. (*Pointing. Everyone listening, wanting to know more.*) When they arrived, they heard of the gold rush. With no money to purchase land and build a home, they set off for the Great White North to join the greatest adventure they ever could have imagined.

FELICITY: That house has been abandoned for years. No one knows what happened to the family that lived there.

SABRINA: What were their names?

SAMUEL: What?

SABRINA: Their names. You haven't mentioned their names yet.

SAMUEL: Francois and Laurette Prive. They were my great-grandparents.

FELICITY: (*Looking at him.*) You never mentioned that was your family's house.

SAMUEL: You never asked.

FELICITY: How could I know? Does Alfred know?

JUSTIN: What? What's the big mystery?

SAMUEL: Nothing. There's no big mystery.

FELICITY: Please. Your last name is Prive.

SABRINA: Really! Tell us more.

SAMUEL: When they arrived in the Yukon, they set up camp. A few weeks after an exploration mission, Francois found what he knew to be a pot of gold in its truest form. He kept it secret even from Laurette until he had finalized all the legal claims. He presented her with a document wrapped in gold lace. In 1899, when all was said and done, they returned to this place and built their home on Lighthouse Point.

SABRINA: That's so interesting. Honey, we'll have to go there and see this house.

FELICITY: Yes, we'll have to see this place. I'm very interested in hearing the rest of this story too, but we need to get home.

SABRINA: Oh, please stay a little while longer. I want to hear the ending.

JUSTIN: Let's sit here. (*Pointing at a long log surrounded by driftwood. They all sit.*)

SAMUEL: After a few years, they had the house of their dreams, two children—one girl, one boy—and a third on the way. It was all perfect, beautiful, wonderful, and frightening all at the same time because Laurette had been quite ill. She had learned that she had a weak heart. Three months after the birth of her son, she died. Francois was devastated.

No one speaks. They all listen intently, completely engrossed and sad.

SAMUEL: A few months later, Francois died. His body was found on the beach, curled up at the place where he and Laurette sat every night to watch the sunset. It was believed he died of a broken heart, too sad ever to recover from the death of his sweetheart.

SABRINA: (*Teary eyes.*) That's so sad.

SAMUEL: (*Takes a deep breath. Playing with a stick, drawing in the sand.*) There was no family to look after the children. Laurette and Francois's last will explicitly stated that the children should never be raised apart. The only person Francois felt he could entrust them to was a woman who lived alone up island, in a cabin. She was a world-renowned artist. You know her work—Patricia Evans. She painted this beautiful West Coast and its animals. Her husband was a fisherman. His ship was lost at sea during a storm. She was widowed before she was thirty. Patricia was a beautiful and extremely humble woman. She raised the three children until they were old enough to care for themselves. All three went on to have wonderful, successful lives, not with financial wealth but in their contributions to others in need. They all had a sense of fulfillment from the gift of giving. Patricia instilled in them the values she knew that their parents wanted them to have. All charitable gifts and donations were made anonymously and with discretion. Patricia followed every instruction Francois left in the will. She lived in the Lighthouse Point house until she died. It became her home, and she was a grandmother to the next generation of the Prive children there. This house had been built on love, and it became a sacred place for the family. Then it fell empty, and no one returned.

JUSTIN: Why? Why has the house been empty for so long?

The sun was getting higher and higher. Felicity looked in the distance for the boat. It was nowhere in sight.

SAMUEL: Like I said, that house was built on love. I'm the last member of the family. My parents couldn't live there for very long because my father was bound to a wheelchair from the age of twenty-one due to a boat accident. I was born in that house, but we had to leave when I was two because my father needed to be closer to a medical facility for daily treatment. He died a year later. A few years later, my mother remarried and moved to England. That year I met Alfred in boarding school.

FELICITY: (*Smiling. She notices the boat coming around the point.*) The house might not be empty for much longer. Let's head back home.

SABRINA: Thanks, Samuel, for sharing that. It's a beautiful love story. Do you think now you'll move back in anytime soon?

SAMUEL: (*Looks out at the sea. He doesn't answer her question but wants to say, "Yes, with my lovely Rose."*) It was lovely to meet you again. We'll see you later.

JUSTIN: See you later. (*To Sabrina.*) Let's go over there. We can rehearse a bit more before we catch up with the others.

FELICITY: Enjoy the rest of your morning. We'll see you later at the house.

SABRINA: See you later.

Sabrina and Justin walk off, Justin with his arm around her, keeping her very close.

FELICITY: Anything else we need to know about you?

SAMUEL: No, that's it. Isn't that enough?

FELICITY: Interesting. Why haven't you told Alfred about the house?

SAMUEL: I'm alone, Felicity. I know I have you guys and other wonderful friends, but in my heart, I'm alone. I want to know that kind of love. When…when I'm forty-five, Felicity, and I'm alone, and I don't like to be reminded…I've been in love with her since the moment I met her…How long ago was that? It's been at least six years.

FELICITY: You were able to talk about it today. It's good that you told us the story. I'll leave it to you to tell Alfred. Be sure to tell him today when he gets back. The kids are going to bring it up, and Alfred won't know what they are going on about. (*She puts her arm around him.*) She'll be home soon enough.

Samuel's awareness of his true self increases the hollow sound, leaving him to contemplate the new possibilities before him. His nightmares, a fraction of his existence, dying in self-defense, permeate the inevitable greatness of his poetic self. A writer will avoid writing at every opportunity while finding every opportunity to write. The trap. Swaggering, provoking, poetic love or just poor timing. Timing? Or God's plan? He looks up at the sky.

FELICITY: (*Shouting, pointing at the Frisbee coming right for Samuel's head.*) Look out! (*It smacks him right on the forehead.*)

SAMUEL: Fuck! (*Rubs his forehead, where a bright red stripe is forming.*) That hurt!

FELICITY: That was the universe's way of snapping you back into the here and now. (*Giggling.*) For the past twenty minutes, you've been deep in that head of yours. I swear it's your favorite place. You all right? (*Giggles, taking him by the arm.*) This way. We're almost home.

SAMUEL: "I will not yield, / To kiss the ground before young Malcolm's feet, / And to be baited with the rabble's curse. / Though Birnam Wood be come to Dunsinane, / And thou opposed, being of no woman born, / Yet I will try the last. Before my body / I throw my warlike shield. Lay on, Macduff, /And damn'd be him that first cries, 'Hold, enough!'" (*Smiles, looking smug.*)

FELICITY: Well, aren't you full of surprises. Who's that? (*They both look ahead. They can see a car pull up at the house.*) Look at that car.

SAMUEL: That's a 1922 Citroen De Convertible.

FELICITY: Hmm. (*Pause.*) It's Eliot.

SAMUEL: Eliot?

FELICTY: Yes, Eliot and Margaret Warthog.

SAMUEL: Oh yeah? Haven't seen them in a while. The alpaca guy.

FELICITY: Yep, that's him.

SAMUEL: He's the one who sent you the manuscript of *Write between the Lines* by Viviane Shoemaker?

FELICITY: (*Surprised. She looks at him.*) Yes. How do you know about that?

SAMUEL: You left it on the kitchen counter. I read it one morning when you were out. Are you going to do it? You'd be crazy not to. It's quite the story. Viviane. Remarkable, wasn't she?

FELICITY: Yes, she was. Come on. (*They pick up their shoes and head back to the house.*)

MARGARET: Hi! (*Shouts, waves at Felicity and Samuel. Then to Eliot.*) Who's that with Felicity? Handsome.

ELIOT: (*Rolls his eyes.*) Samuel. Alfred's childhood friend. The eccentric millionaire I told you about.

MARGARET: Oh yeah.

Felicity and Samuel arrive at the house. They brush the sand from their clothes and put their shoes back on.

FELICITY: Hi. Welcome. (*She hugs both Eliot and Margaret, kisses them both on the cheeks.*) You remember Samuel?

ELIOT: Yes, of course. (*The men shake hands.*) Good seeing you again.

SAMUEL: Likewise.

ELIOT: My wife, Margaret.

SAMUEL: Yes, I remember. (*Kisses Margaret on the cheek.*)

FELICITY: Nice car.

ELIOT: Got her last year. Last trip out of the year.

MARGARET: Georgette will be arriving later today. We're so excited. It's all last-minute. We weren't expecting her for at least another six months. I called Alfred this morning to tell him we'd be coming by soon, and I told him that Georgette is coming back home and that she caught up with Rose in Guinea.

FELICITY: (*Evasive.*) Alfred is out on the boat. He should be back anytime now. Let's go in the house.

ELIOT: (*Takes Felicity by the arm.*) You're looking good, as usual. It's good to see you, Felicity.

SAMUEL: Margaret, come in. What can I get you? Tea, coffee, hot chocolate…

Samuel and Margaret walk ahead, enter the house. Felicity and Eliot lag behind.

FELICITY: Good to see you as well. (*Takes his arm. Rests her head on his shoulder.*) How's your favorite lady?

ELIOT: Henrietta is doing just fine. (*They laugh.*)

FELICITY: Margaret looks good as well. I hear she's been busy.

ELIOT: Yes. She's completed two movies this year and is starting a third. (*They sit on the porch steps.*) I've missed you. We've missed you.

Do you have any idea what's going on? Why Georgette is coming home sooner than expected?

FELICITY: I'm sure she'll tell us all about it. We have the entire weekend to catch up with everyone.

ELIOT: Jack.

FELICITY: I read the manuscript.

ELIOT: He's anxious to see you as well. You've not seen each other since Luc's funeral. How have you been?

SAMUEL: (*Comes out to the porch with two cups in his hands.*) Here you go. Hot chocolate. Margaret and I will start preparing brunch. Margaret is in love with Matilda. We'll have to check her bag when you go. We may have a missing cat by the end of the weekend.

They giggle.

FELICITY: Thank you. Wonderful.

Samuel goes back into the house.

FELICITY: Rose will be here as well. She's coming back. Seems like everyone will be here this weekend. We have everything ready for the barbecue tonight. It's been great at the school.

ELIOT: I got your letter. Rose—wow. Never thought she'd come back to us as well. I read the manuscript you sent. *Tulip.* Interesting. Your students did a great job.

FELICITY: You can tell them when you meet them. They'll be coming by the house later today. The show starts at sunset, and then we'll have the barbecue at the house, followed by a bonfire on the beach.

ELIOT: Sounds like a lovely evening. Who's that? (*Looks ahead in the distance at two people standing at the end of the drive.*)

FELICITY: Who?

ELIOT: Over there. (*Pointing in front of him.*)

FELICITY: I can't tell who it is.

The two figures in the distance approach, their silhouettes revealing that one is male and the other female. They're wearing backpacks.

FELICITY: Oh my God!

ELIOT: You know them? (*Sips his hot chocolate.*)

FELICITY: So should you. Well, one of them, anyway.

Before she can say another word, Eliot drops his cup and runs as fast as he can toward them.

ELIOT: (*Shouts.*) Margaret! Margaret, get out here!

MARGARET: (*Runs out of the house.*) What's all the shouting about? Where's he going? He's going to have a heart attack if he keeps running like that.

Felicity stands, points in the direction of the two people walking up the drive.

MARGARET: Our baby! (*She walks out to meet them. Surprised. Overwhelmed by joy.*)

SAMUEL: (*Comes out on the porch.*) Where's my sous chef going? Who's that? More mystery guests?

FELICITY: That's Georgette, their daughter, and the other, I'm guessing, is for you.

Samuel goes weak at the knees. Holds himself up by leaning on the porch railing.

FELICITY: Well. We're in for an interesting weekend. Samuel. Samuel. (*Taps him on the shoulder.*)

SAMUEL: You don't say. I should go over there with them, shouldn't I? (*He's unable to move. Felicity takes the dishcloth from his hands.*)

FELICITY: Go. (*Kisses his shoulder.*)

SAMUEL: I…(*Time slows, almost reversing, feet off the ground, drifting. His mind reflecting on all the details, entranced by the vision, fixated on the linear view of a recurring dream, an epic moment.*)

Eliot embraces Georgette. Margaret weeps with joy, joins the embrace.

CHERIF: Samuel. (*Face to face. Samuel, unable to speak, stares at Cherif, looking at him from head to toe, touching his face. Samuel wraps his arms around him, tears rolling down his face quietly. The eternal hug.*)

Felicity walks down the drive to greet them. Margaret and Eliot look at Samuel, perplexed, and look at Georgette with intrigue.

MARGARET: Honey, sweetheart, who's your friend?

GEORGETTE: Mom, this is Cherif. He's from Guinea. Cherif, my parents, Eliot and Margaret.

CHERIF: (*Samuel releases him. Cherif puts out his hand.*) Mr. and Mrs. Warthog, pleasure to finally meet you. Georgette has told me so much about you.

ELIOT: (*He and Margaret both give him a hug.*) Nice to meet you as well, Cherif.

MARGARET: Guinea. How did you come to meet our lovely Georgette?

GEORGETTE: Mom, we'll tell you about it this weekend.

MARGARET: Are you with us for a while?

GEORGETTE: Mom, Dad.

SAMUEL: Ah, Felicity.

CHERIF: Felicity, our host. Felicity, Cherif.

FELICITY: (*Shakes hands with Cherif, gives him a kiss on the cheek.*) Nice to meet you. Welcome to our home, Georgette. (*Hugs her.*) Wonderful to see you as well. It's good to have you home.

GEORGETTE: Felicity, it's so lovely to see you again. How are you?

FELICITY: I'm good. Well, let's all go to the house. Alfred should be arriving anytime now.

Everyone starts walking toward the house. Eliot takes Georgette's backpack.

GEORGETTE: Mom, Dad. (*She stops walking. Takes Cherif by the hand. Everyone stops, looks at them.*) Yes, Cherif will be staying with us awhile. Forever, actually. We're engaged. (*No one says a word. Georgette moves closer to Cherif.*)

MARGARET: Engaged! That's...that's wonderful news, honey. Welcome to the family, Cherif. (*She embraces them both.*)

GEORGETTE: Dad.

ELIOT: Honey. (*Teary eyes.*) Congratulations. (*Gives them both big hugs.*) I'm very happy for you both. Welcome to the family, Cherif.

FELICITY: Congratulations to you both. (*Gives them each a kiss.*)

SAMUEL: Yes, congratulations are definitely in order. (*Puts out his hand.*)

ALFRED: (*Standing in front of the porch. Shouting. Waving.*) Hi! Hey! What are you all doing over there? (*Starts walking toward them.*)

The others walk toward Alfred. Introductions are made. Alfred greets Georgette as if she is his own daughter whom he hasn't seen for years. The others share the good news. Lots of embraces, handshakes, and congratulations. Once everyone is inside, Alfred gives them a grand tour of the house and property, including the beach area. Sabrina, Justin, Jason, and Arnold join everyone at the beach house. Brunch is served. It's a perfect day.

Sabrina, Justin, Jason, and Arnold head off to the theater house. Rose's flight is delayed. Jack calls Eliot to tell him they won't be there in time to see the play, but to go ahead and they would meet them at the house afterward. Samuel reveals nothing, reveals everything. The play, The Man Who Said Nothing, *starring Arnold Winters and Sabrina Wright, is a hit.*

After the show, everyone returns to the beach house. Mrs. Hitchcock arrives with an assortment of gourmet baked goods. The property is beautifully decorated with twinkling hanging lights and candles. Everyone is outside eating, drinking, singing, and dancing around the fire. Samuel looks out onto the beach. A ghost is walking on the beach. He approaches.

Felicity walks around to the front of the house to get the remaining baked goods from Mrs. Hitchcock's car. A Land Rover is parked next to Mrs. Hitchcock's car. Felicity stops in her tracks. Jack steps out of the Land Rover.

Samuel approaches the ghost.

SAMUEL: Rose!

FELICITY: Jack! (*He approaches Felicity. Takes her by the hand and kisses it. She puts her head on his chest, releasing all her sorrow.*)

The End

www.ingramcontent.com/pod-product-compliance
Ingram Content Group UK Ltd.
Pitfield, Milton Keynes, MK11 3LW, UK
UKHW040708160925
7921UKWH00013B/137